THE LAND OF PROMISES

(CITY ON THE SEA SERIES BOOK 3)

HEATHER CARSON

All Rights Reserved.

Copyright © 2021 Heather Carson

Courtesy of Blue Tuesday Books

Cover Design by Fay Lane at faylane.com

ISBN: 9798736954988

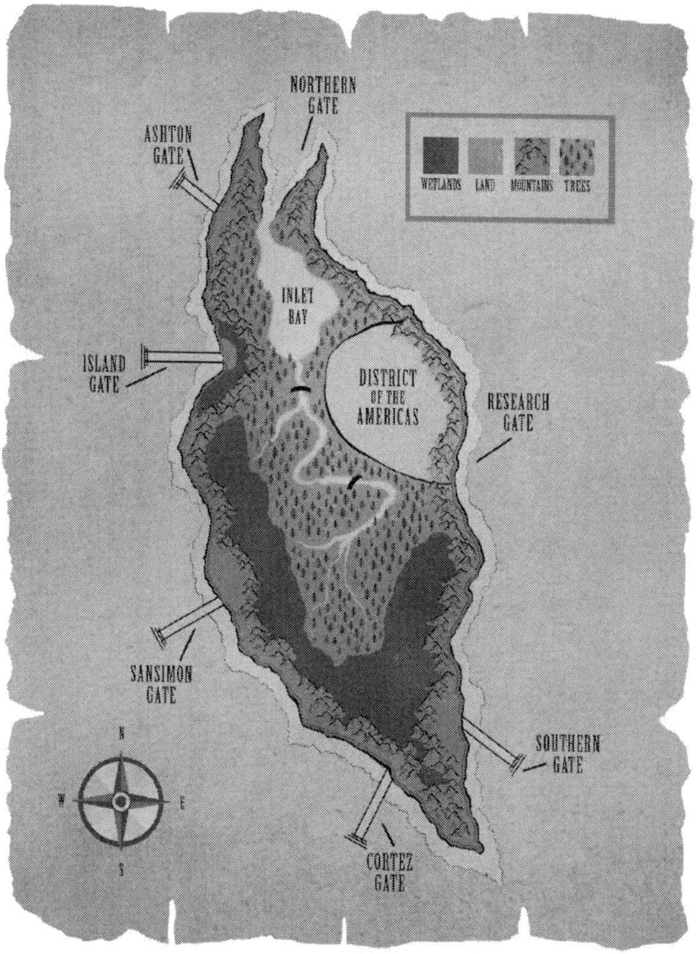
NORTHERN GATE
ASHTON GATE
WETLANDS
LAND
MOUNTAINS
TREES
INLET BAY
ISLAND GATE
DISTRICT OF THE AMERICAS
RESEARCH GATE
SANSIMON GATE
N
W
E
S
SOUTHERN GATE
CORTEZ GATE

☦ CHAPTER ONE ☦

The paper is still in my pocket. I run my hand down the front of my seal skin dress to make sure of it, and cling to that one truth as I'm led into the early morning light of this foreign world. Everything I know is fifty miles away, yet it feels so distant that it shatters my heart. This world is a lie. If I can find a way to escape it somehow, then I know the paper will show me the way home.

"Sorry about that." The rude nurse who judged my appearance last night wraps her arm around my shoulders and guides me down the hall. *Rosemary,* her name is Rosemary, and she isn't as rude as I thought.

When Calder's mother burst into the room- *oh gods, I'm still cringing at the recent memory*- Rosemary rushed to my defense, explaining how I'd dragged him for miles on a makeshift stretcher and saved his life. Mother Morgana Auburn, High Council Leader of the District of the Americas, regarded me coldly. Despite my concern for that stupid watchman, I was grateful that Rosemary pulled me away.

"We'll take care of him," the not rude nurse reassures me now. "Let's get you to the Welcome Center."

"I was just coming to see if she needed another ride." The mother from the boulder house I visited last night meets us in the long hallway. Her husband Charles stands behind her, looking at his feet and casting glances up at me from under his graying eyelashes. It isn't the first time that I've wondered if something is wrong with him.

"I'll walk her over there," Rosemary says. "You've done so much already, Mother Neil. Why don't you go home and get some rest?"

Mother Neil. I store this new information along with every other thing I've learned tonight. "Thank you for helping me."

"Oh, dear girl." Mother Neil smiles. "You are the hero today."

*

Rosemary shivers as the wind hits us outside of the building that they call a hospital. Her sharp nose crinkles as a yawn distorts her porcelain face. I've never seen skin as clear as hers. It matches the blinding white uniform perfectly. *She needs to see the sun.*

"Sorry about that." She covers her mouth as if embarrassed. "I've been working the night shift for the past few months and still haven't gotten used to it."

"Why are you sorry?" I study her face, not understanding. "Are you sorry that you are tired?"

"Never mind." She gives me a small smile. "This must be so overwhelming. But the Welcome Center will help."

I pull my father's jacket closed over my chest trying to block out the wind. "Are there more people from my city at the Welcome Center?"

"Oh I don't know," Rosemary laughs as she begins walking down the path. "There are so many cities out there. It's hard to keep track of who comes from where."

The path is smooth and raised. It's nothing like the beaten path we walked on through the mountains. Once I'm sure that I'm not going to trip, I look up to see this new world around me.

The sun's rays are richly golden, illuminating brownish fields of grass. The light is so soft that the world seems dreamlike and lost in a hazy fog of early morning glow. There are paths out in the fields. Some lead to giant white boulders like the hospital and Mother Neil's residence.

"How do you move the large rocks for your buildings?" I ask as I study the neat rows that stretch through the valley. There's no way these boulders were here naturally in this pattern.

"Rocks?" Rosemary turns to look at what I'm seeing. "Huh, I guess they do sort of look like rocks. Funny, I never thought that. They are geodomes, well monolithic domes… geodesic biodomes… I'm honestly not quite sure what the technical term is. We just call them domes. But they aren't made from rocks. It's a solar panel outer layer that absorbs energy from the sun and powers our electricity."

The words she speaks come to me like whale calls under the ocean. My forehead creases as I stare at her. "What?"

"Don't worry." Rosemary laughs as she laces her arm through mine. The action makes my muscles tense, but she doesn't seem to notice and continues to pull me forward. "They'll be able to explain it better at the Welcome Center."

*

The Welcome Center is what they call a dome. It's a little bigger than the hospital. As I approach, I run my fingers across the side. The material feels like fiberglass and as the sun moves further above the mountains in the distance it reflects a shimmering water type effect on the panels that line the building.

"I'll come check on you in a few days." Rosemary yawns as we near the entrance. The thought of her leaving worries me. *Everything about this place worries me.*

"Will you let me know when Calder wakes?" I ask.

"Of course I will." Her eyes light up like we are sharing some sort of secret and she winks playfully. "You'll be the first to know."

It would be cute if I cared enough to think she was a friend. *But she was nice,* I remind myself. *Despite the look she gave me when I arrived.* She'd said my clothes were dirty and they couldn't allow me into a sterile room.

I bite my lip a little too hard as I force myself to giggle, playing into whatever game she has started. "Thank you. I'm worried about him."

"I bet." She reaches for the door and opens it for me. "I'd never work that hard for a watchman unless I somehow cared for him."

Her words confuse me and I hesitate before stepping inside. "Do you not like the watchmen either?"

"Not exactly." She shrugs her shoulders. "They just seem so dirty and wild until they end their service contract."

I want to speak with her further, to pry the truths of this world from her lips, but a woman as tall and strong as Beau walks toward us from inside the dome.

"Mother Wolfe." Rosemary nods. "I've brought your new arrival." The mother, *yet another mother,* stretches her arms out wide.

"Welcome child," she calls to me. "What a journey you must have had. These are very unusual circumstances, but you made it to us safely just the same. My goodness, you must be hungry. Let's get you something to eat. Close the door, Rosemary, you're letting out all the warm air."

Before I know it, Mother Wolfe has smothered me in her embrace. I try to look over the white clothed arm that squishes my nose, but the door is closed and Rosemary is already gone.

"Now, I know you have questions." Mother Wolfe smiles sympathetically.

I inhale deeply to suck in enough oxygen for all the words that want to rush from my mouth, but Mother Wolfe stops me before I can even start.

"Later." She pats my hand. Her skin is soft and smooth despite the wrinkles that come with age. She gently leads me around a partition, deeper into the silent dome. "There's so much to tell you. We have a specifically designed program just for you to learn about your new home, but it takes a few weeks. We've found it is better to give this information in strategic chunks so as not to overwhelm you. But I promise the process isn't painful. This is a new and better life than the one you are accustomed to."

"No." Anger creeps its way up my spine and sends flashes of heat rolling over my skin. My feet stop moving as images fill my mind of Calder's 'one question for every mile I walk' torturous game. "I want to know all of it. Now."

Mother Wolfe pauses and arches a perfectly shaped eyebrow in my direction. "Oh dear. I assumed you were civil from Mother Neil's report when she called from the hospital. I wasn't ready for another one like you just this soon."

Civil? The anger dissipates and a shiver runs through my body as the weight of the night catches up to me. *She must think I'm a barbarian.* "I apologize for my outburst. I'm so unbelievably tired. But I need answers. More than anything, I need the truth."

"And you'll get the truth." She regains her perfect smile. The white of her teeth matches the color of her clothes and hair.

"What other one?" I sigh as I fall in step beside her. This is what she wants. Her whole demeanor lightens as I lower my voice and follow.

"What do you mean?" She turns to glance over her shoulder.

"You said another one just like me." I try not to look at her as I speak. This world is strange. I wish I knew the rules already so I can understand what they want from me.

"Oh, that." Mother Wolfe sucks her lip between her teeth. "It's nothing. There is a…"

"This food is bland!"

Mother Wolfe's words are cut short by a commotion in the room we enter. Long rows of tables and chairs fill the main space. The far wall is lined with a glass enclosure steamed up by the smell of food. My stomach growls just as the sound of a plate being slammed against the table echoes through the room.

"I'm sorry." She turns to me, her eyes wide in horror, but I'm already running past her.

"Jillian!" I cry out her name as my heart simultaneously swells and breaks.

"Brooke?" She pulls in deep breaths as her shoulders shake. "Oh gods, how did this happen?"

I collide into her outstretched arms as tears stream down my face and sobs rock my entire body. Jillian doesn't cry, but her strong hands smoothing back my hair shake against my head.

"How? Why?" she whispers.

"I don't know." My tears soak the smock she wears, turning it a darker shade of gray.

"I take it you two know each other?" Mother Wolfe coughs beside us. I turn to nod just as Jillian places a protective arm in front of me.

"This is unusual," Mother Wolfe continues. "Let me consult the council on this, but I don't see any harm in it now. In fact, it might do our Jillian here some good."

Jillian tenses beside me, but remains silent. She's assessing the situation too.

"Yes." Mother Wolfe smiles brightly. "I think this will be a good thing. After breakfast, Jillian dear, why don't you show Brooke to her room? She'll be in number 14."

Mother Wolfe nods her head excitedly, her white bun bobbing up and down. "This is a good thing," she reassures herself as she begins to walk away. "Oh and Brooke…" She pauses just as Jillian and I clasp hands. "We haven't gotten the official report from the watchmen yet. What is it you do?"

"I do?" The question has so many answers. I'm not sure which one to grab. Mother Wolfe chews the inside of her cheek.

"What did they decide to take you away from that place for?" she finally asks. *Does that question sound as awful to her as it does to me?*

I shake my head, not fully understanding the correct response. "I can paint likenesses."

"Fascinating." Her eyes light up as she claps her hands together. "I can't wait to see them."

*

Jillian's words are a rushing tide that fills the quiet room with life. "The food is disgusting," she tells me as an elderly man dressed in white pants and shirt hands me a plate of breakfast from behind the glass. "The people are weak," she explains as more of them enter, dressed in the same light-gray colored clothes as the smock she is wearing. Most don't acknowledge my presence, but the few that do eye me distrustfully.

"This is insane," she exhales as she takes the seat beside me at the table. "How can this be possible? How does a place like this exist?"

I swallow a bite of the scrambled eggs and it gets stuck in my throat. She's right, this food needs salt. "Don't they tell you all this in whatever the program is that Mother Wolfe talked about?"

"She's not my mother." Jillian throws her fork down in disgust. "Wolfe is right, they do try to tell you. But none of this makes sense." Her eyes are pleading, begging me for an answer when I'm not even sure this all is real. "How does this place exist?"

"I don't know." The lights in the room are suddenly overwhelming. Everything is too bright, too quiet. The lump of eggs slides heavily into my stomach as if I'd swallowed a rock. I clutch my side and close my eyes while the entire world spins.

"Are you alright?" Jillian cries as she reaches for my hand.

One breath… Two breaths… I can figure out a way to fix this. The words in my head are spoken through my father's voice as he stands on the uninhabitable rocky outcropping. It's my grandmother's voice as she tucks a lock of hair behind my ear. It's Meghan's voice, holding me behind a barricaded door while our mother screams. I think them again and again until it sounds like my own voice.

"Brooke," Jillian says softly. "What's wrong?"

"Everything." I blink as the room comes back into focus. "A place like this should not exist."

"That's what I'm saying," she sighs in relief. "But none of these morons will listen to me."

"Okay." I take another steadying breath. "What have you tried so far?"

"Everything I can think of." She picks up her fork and uses the tongs to push the food around on her plate. Her other hand makes a clenched fist under the table. "Now I'm just resorting to being a pain in the ass."

I snicker through my nose. That's definitely not what anyone I know would do. Jillian has always been rebellious- the exact thing we were taught not to be. My heart aches for the loss of my people, but hardens when I realize they need to know the truth.

"Are you worried about causing trouble?" My eyes dart to the servers dressed in white, the rest of the people in the room wear gray. Plastered smiles light up their faces as they ladle the tasteless eggs onto plates.

"No." Jillian leans back in her chair and folds her arms over her chest. "I'm too important to them so they have to put up with me."

"What do you mean, important?" I push the plate aside, no longer hungry.

"You remember my mother Vera, right?" She continues as I nod, "She never retired, she just told me she did. They brought her here instead."

"Why?" I always wondered why she chose to leave when her aquaponics system did so well, but she was a hard worker and deserved retirement. My fork clatters onto the discarded plate. *No one deserves to retire.*

"I'll have to explain it when I take you there." Jillian stands and I follow her out of the dining area.

"Are we allowed to go wherever we want?" I stare at the walls that line the hallway. It's disorientating to work out how walls this straight fit into a structure so round. I try not to focus on it too hard. Everything that has happened since last night is making me dizzy.

"Sort of," Jillian says. "We aren't technically citizens until we earn our whites, but we are allowed to leave if we want. Most of us work outside the Welcome Center but we spend our free time here."

I check over my shoulder to make sure we are alone. "What's stopping you from running away?"

She lowers her eyes, studying her own feet as if they betrayed her. "Let's get you to your room. You've dealt with enough already today."

✝ CHAPTER TWO ✝

The curved window in Room 14 has a thick layer of glass that blocks the breeze from dancing inside. There is a lock in the middle which holds it in place. I check to make sure it can open.

A thick material lines the floor. I remove my boots and socks, wiggling my toes deep within the fibrous strands. It cushions my feet in a comforting way that relieves the pain of walking for so long.

A box like a free-standing closet opens wide to reveal a full length, uncracked mirror. Inside hangs a row of gray dresses identical to the ones that Jillian wears. I run my fingers over the material of the clothes. It's delicate and thin.

The second door swings open to a washroom. I turn the silver knobs and warm water pours out. It's shocking, but not too unpleasant. The water I've always known is cold, pumped up from the sea through our rusted pipes while the waste is pushed away through crude aqueducts under the ocean. I wonder where this waste goes as I look at the giant bathtub. We don't have tubs this big. It would take up too much space. The entire washroom itself is as big as Meghan's kitchen.

Meghan. The memory of her face turns my legs into jellyfish. I fall hard against the floor, clutching at my chest and attempting to wrench my heart from it.

The tears fall freely now that I'm alone in this strange room. She's going crazy without me there. I just know it. I can picture her with wild hair and bloodshot eyes, forcing Rowan to question everyone in order to find out what happened. I hope she's able to sleep. I hope Zander and Thora are okay. *Gods, I hope she saw my mural.*

If she saw it then she'd know what happened. But even if she didn't, there's bound to be rumors. Word travels fast in the city. I only wish she could have seen the words telling her I love her.

I sit shaking on the cold floor, my breath hitching in my lungs, until a heavy numbness consumes me. Then I force myself into the tub. A spray of warm water shoots out from a pipe above and my eyes open wide in panic. I wrestle the paper from my pocket, tossing it safely onto the stone slab flooring of the washroom, before letting the water wash away the grime of the last few days.

Once my dress is rinsed and wrung out, I hang it on the bar overhead. I wash my bare skin tenderly so as not to damage the blisters and bruises I've accumulated. The warm water never seems to end and I stand under it entirely too long as it eases the tension from my muscles.

Soft white cloths are in the washroom cabinet. I wrap one around my body and the fibers instantly wick away the moisture on my skin. It's an odd feeling, but not awful.

There's a wooden chair and table in the corner, but I go to the bed instead. White blankets hug the mattress tightly. I rip at the folds until they come loose and slide naked into them. The sensation is so comforting that it relaxes every part of my body. It takes only seconds until I drift away on this soft white cloud of sleep.

*

The clouds are gray before a coming storm. A sickening shade of pale gray like the hue of deceased faces. Like the color of Jillian's smock. I'm surrounded by it, falling- no drowning in wisps of fog. I thrash out my arms trying to find something to grasp. But there's nothing to cling to this high in the sky, nothing solid to help me stay upright.

I twist my body around, ready to face the substance that will embrace my descent. The deep blue ocean stretches out before me, untamed and expansive. I'll die when I smack against the water. No one can survive a fall from this height. But at least I'll get to feel the waves again. One more time, I'll get to taste the salt on my tongue and feel the thousand lashes as her frigid fingers wrap around my body.

A feeling of peace consumes me, but I force my eyes to open before I touch the sea. *No. Not yet.*

*

The sun illuminates the pristine room and I blink my eyes as they adjust to it. There's no rust in here. No aging metal corroded by salty air. It feels too clean, like I stain the walls with just my presence.

The white blankets are twisted around my body in knots. I untangle myself from their embrace and sit up, pulling my knees to my chest. I didn't mean to fall asleep but exhaustion overtook me. Now that I can focus again, I need to make a plan.

At least Jillian is here. That thought brings me some relief. I'm not all alone, but this still isn't good enough. I have to warn them. I have to tell Meghan. She can never set foot on that retirement ship. No one can. They have to know about this place and I need to find a way to do that.

Through the open door of the washroom, I see Calder's paper discarded on the floor where I left it. I scramble off the bed, my heart pounding in my chest, and quickly hide it between my folded hands. *How stupid was I to leave it there?* My eyes dart around the room but no one comes bursting through the door. I unfold it and study the lines once more, committing them to memory before sliding it underneath the box closet.

My clothes are still wet. I debate on dressing in them anyway but the sensible part of me knows I need to look the part. I need to bide my time and try to understand. I need to listen and play along. This is what I'm good at. I always have been. And even without the paper, I still know I can find my way home. Worst case scenario, I'll leave without them expecting it.

My footsteps are too loud as they echo down the quiet halls. I'd assume that a welcome center would be a little more welcoming and not quite this empty. The smooth fabric of the gray dress clings to the curves of my body much like the blankets on the bed did. I fold my arms over my chest, feeling unnaturally exposed despite the thin coverage.

"You're awake!" Mother Wolfe exclaims as I surprise her at the desk near the entrance of the dome. Her voice has a happy singsong quality that I hadn't noticed this morning. "We expected you to sleep until tomorrow," she laughs. "I already made arrangements to have dinner brought to your room."

"Why?" The word slips from my lips before I can stop it.

"You had a long journey." She eyes me quizzically. "You need your sleep and you need to eat."

"No," I whisper, shaking my head. "Why are you being this nice to me?"

"Oh, dear child." Her blue eyes fill with tears. "I know it's hard to understand just now, but you'll see. Life is much different here than it is in the cities outside the wall."

I'm confused. "Have you lived in the cities on the sea?"

"Oh goodness no." She places a hand over her heart. "But I've heard enough to know that no talented young woman deserves that kind of life."

Her words are a sword, but her eyes are soft and full of pity. She truly believes what she says. Anger boils in my stomach, but I swallow down my pride, locking it somewhere deep and out of reach.

"Is Jillian here?" I ask.

"No." Mother Wolfe shakes her head. "She's gone to work, but will be back this evening. It's a miracle you came to us. She left the center today without a fight or a single snide remark. I'm utterly convinced it is a blessing you are here, despite the odd circumstances."

I chew my lip as she speaks, unsure of what to do with myself now. There must be some work to be done, but I'll be damned if I know what they want from me.

"How are you feeling?" Mother Wolfe smiles, sensing my hesitation. "Are you up for a tour of the Welcome Center?"

*

The square walls fit too perfectly beneath the circular roof. Most of the building is illuminated by the sun peeking through the panels of the far away ceiling. I could easily get lost in here. It reminds me of the spiraling walkways around the docks, except I can't see what's on the other side of these walls.

"You've already been to the cafeteria." Mother Wolfe walks slowly. I wish she'd move a little faster.

"The cafe-what?" I ask.

"Where you receive your meals." She tries to hide her smile. "Anytime you are hungry, just head down there and the cooks will fix you something to eat. But they serve three common meals a day."

The place I ate breakfast is like the tavern. This I understand.

"And over here is what we call a library. It holds all the books you will need to understand the world," Mother Wolfe says this dismissively as we pass the open doors of a room that seems to fill the center of the dome. "But don't worry about that now. In time, you'll be taught to read letters and then you can peruse the books at your leisure."

Letters. Books. Reading… My feet stop moving and I am frozen in front of the doors that lead to what they call a library. These words are so foreign in my world, yet they roll off her tongue as quick as an eel darting between the coral.

"I already know how to read." My heart hammers against my rib cage. "Can I look at the books now?"

"Oh dear." The color drains from her face as if trying to match the hue of her robes and hair. "You are full of surprises, aren't you?"

She studies me for so long that I squirm in my own skin. *Did I make the right decision in admitting that?* Henry and Calder already know, so it was just a matter of time before she was told the truth. I'm not so sure why this matters, but it seems to shock everyone from this world.

I make a quick decision to own it and raise my chin. "I'm not trying to be difficult, but I do know how to read. Will I be allowed in here when I want or should I wait for your approval and to finish the program first?"

"You can come whenever you like!" Mother Wolfe exclaims. "After the morning discussion the reading lessons begin. If you feel confident in your abilities then let the instructor know that you'll be heading to the library. Truthfully, this is the hardest obstacle to overcome. If you know how to read then you are already light years ahead of your peers."

I stand still for a moment, staring into the room that holds meters upon meters of small boxes on shelves, trying to decipher the meaning behind her words.

"Are you coming, dear?" she calls back to me. I peel myself from the sight of it all and hurry to catch up.

"Where do you get the paper?" I slow down to match her pace.

"What paper?" When she is confused her eyebrow curves in a perfect circle like the domes.

"The paper for books." I try not to let my frustration turn my tone sour. *My father already told me about books. They needed lots and lots of paper.*

"Oh, I see." She continues to walk. "Some of the books are ancient. You'll be able to tell because the pages are laminated, er, wrapped in a clear and thin plastic. Long ago, they cut down trees to make that type of paper."

A gasp involuntarily rushes from my mouth.

"Barbaric, wasn't it?" She wraps a comforting arm around my shoulder. "Now we grow a plant called hemp, blending the fibers into a pulp, and make our paper from that. It's much better for the environment."

She seems so pleased with this explanation, that I don't have the heart to tell her I don't see much of a difference. I stare at my feet as we travel deeper into the dome, trying to absorb as much as I can about this new world.

"Why do so many women call themselves mothers?" I ask.

"Well, we are all mothers." She smiles politely. "But it is also a mark of distinction. The High Council of Mothers has been taking care of the earth for generations. After the wars and the destruction, the first mother stepped forward and demanded peace. Our entire society is based on a matriarchal hierarchy and we celebrate female characteristics. But those we specifically call Mother hold a position on the council."

"The council runs your world?" I try to wade through this new information.

"Not exactly," Mother Wolfe sighs. "Your instructor will probably explain this better than I can. We don't really run the world. We just vote to decide on best practices and rules to keep our society a peaceful one."

I bite my lip as we continue to walk, also failing to understand this difference.

"Is the council all women?" I ask quietly.

"Of course." She directs me down a hall to our right. "Men are far too irrational to work in harmony. History has taught us that much."

I want to refute her response, but she opens a door that leads to a room with light so blinding it forces me to step back.

"Oh dear, I'm sorry," she apologizes. "The first few days of artificial lighting are hard for some people with sensitive eyes. It's easy to forget that when most adjust so quickly. In just a little while, the light will be as natural to you as the sun."

"What's artificial lighting?" I shield my eyes from the glare with my hand.

"That I cannot explain," Mother Wolfe chuckles as she walks into the room. "But luckily for you, we have one of the smartest instructors in the district assigned to us this year."

"Sister Auburn," Mother Wolfe calls out as I follow her into the room. "This is Brooke. She's our new citizen in training."

"I heard she was coming." Sister Auburn stands from her desk, sending a cascade of papers sliding from a stack as her elbow crashes against it. She catches them before they fall to the floor and hurries to straighten the pile. Then she smiles at us with reddened cheeks while tucking a mess of mousy brown, curly hair behind her ears.

I blink hard, trying to focus as the light plays tricks on my eyes. Sister Auburn has the sharp eyebrows and cheek bones of her mother, but the chin and ears of her brother. I choke on my own spit as my heart drops into my stomach. *Calder has a sister.*

☦ CHAPTER THREE ☦

"Are you related to Mother Auburn?" My voice is an inaudible squeak.

"Yes," she smiles playfully, amused at my response. *She also has his mouth.* "And Calder is my younger brother."

"Why do they call you sister?" This question seems stupid. I feel stupid for asking it.

"I'm a Mother-in-training." She raises her strong chin proudly.

"Do Sisters replace their Mothers in the council?" I wish I would shut up. *Why are the words just spilling from me now?* It's jarring to see Calder's face on a woman. I didn't even know he had a sister. My cheeks burn hot as I remember yelling on the rocky outcropping, degrading him for the way he treated women as if he'd never been around one in his life.

"Oh no." Sister Auburn shakes her head. "My mother is the High Council Leader. It's a position of honor and is voted on. I'm apprenticing for the Education Board Council in hopes that one day I will do some good there."

"Your mother, Calder's mother, leads this world of yours?" I gulp.

"She doesn't really lead." Sister Auburn gives me a patient smile. "It's a democratic society. Everyone has a say, but her opinion is highly valued and she makes the final decision in the event of a tie."

A sharp humming comes from the pocket of Mother Wolfe's dress, startling me in this already surreal experience. She pulls out a box that makes the noise and places it against her ear. I stare at her waiting for the meaning of this to make sense.

"Oh dear," she sighs, placing the device back where it came from. "It seems I'm needed at the front desk. Sister Auburn, would you mind showing our Brooke here back to her room? I haven't finished the tour and I don't want her to get lost."

I turn to protest, I can find my way back, but Mother Wolfe is gone quicker than I've seen her move all day. I can't dwell on the old woman's speed for too long because Sister Auburn, *Calder's sister,* is watching me so intently that I'm forced to face her.

"So…" My tongue decides to fail me now and I desperately search for words to fill the awkward silence. "Have you been to see Calder yet?"

"I saw him this morning." Her eyes shift down and she fiddles with the papers on the desk. "They said you saved him. Thank you for that."

Her sudden discomfort matches my own in a way that makes me cringe. I can't for the life of me understand her anxiety, but I don't want her to act this way. *And you don't want to make a bad impression,* the thought takes me by surprise.

"No need to thank me." I smile. "Anyone would have done the same. Is he awake yet?"

"No." She shakes her head and turns to look out the window. "They don't expect him to wake up for a few days."

This worries me. He'll need to get up and eat to get his strength back, but his own sister doesn't seem too concerned, so maybe they do things differently in that hospital of theirs. It makes sense, this whole world is weird.

"Are you alright?" Her voice is soft. I didn't realize she was staring at me.

"I'm fine," I lie. *Nothing about this is fine.*

"I guess you must be worried about him." She sighs as if what she is about to say pains her. "How long have you two been together?"

"We've been traveling together for five days." I glance around the room, eager to avoid her gaze. There are rows of small tables and chairs all lined up perfectly to fill the space.

"Oh no," she giggles nervously. "I mean, how long have you two been romantically involved together?"

My jaw drops to the floor. "There is nothing romantic about him."

"I don't need to know the details." Her face blanches as she claps her hands over her ears and shudders. "Forget that I asked. It's none of my business."

"There are no details to know." I stare at her, mortified. "Why would you think we were romantically involved with each other?"

"You're not?" Her hands slowly drop to her sides as I shake my head. "I'm so sorry. I just assumed. Usually when a watchman comes home with a young female, that's the case."

"What?" Her words make my stomach churn. "Are you saying there are women here that choose to leave the city and be romantic with a watchman?"

"Normally they get married and have a family." She shrugs. "It hasn't happened in a while, but it does happen." She speaks this wistfully, like it's a fairy tale she heard as a child.

The thought of this disgusts me. *How could anyone abandon their families and knowingly become a part of this lie?* I struggle to keep my expression blank.

Her entire posture relaxes as she moves out from behind the desk, coming over to shake my hand. "My apologies. I was just hurt because Calder never mentioned anything to me. Then you showed up and I didn't know what to say."

"No need to apologize." I squeeze her soft hand gently, not wanting to crush it, before letting go. "Any sister would feel the same. I take it you two are close."

"I think so." She smiles, nodding her head. "Well, as close as a brother and sister can be anyway. I haven't heard from him in a few weeks though."

Weeks without talking to someone doesn't seem that close to me. But then again, this isn't my world. "How often do the watchmen get to come home? Maybe he's just been busy."

"They aren't allowed back until their contract is up." Her eyes open wide in alarm. "But normally he calls from ship or at least writes a letter."

"Which letter?" My head cocks to the side.

"Oh goodness." She places a hand over her mouth. "I'm getting ahead of myself. We try not to use foreign words or phrases with citizens-in-training until they can put them into context. But don't worry, we'll take as long as you need to figure it out and I will be right here every step of the way."

I shrug off her misplaced concern. "I know what letters are, I'm only trying to figure out what letter he sends you and how that helps you to hear from him."

"You know what letters are?" Her eyebrows raise. "Do you know how to read?"

Why is everyone so fascinated by this? "Yes. I know how to read."

"Oh, okay." She nods, but she doesn't seem convinced. "You'll be my advanced student. A letter is what we call a form of correspondence. It's a message written with many letters on a piece of paper that gets delivered to another person."

I think of the paper Calder slipped underneath my bedroom door the night that I smacked Drake. A letter is made of many letters. *You'd think they'd be more creative with the name.*

"Is that why they saved you?" she asks.

"Saved me?" The question bothers me, but she doesn't seem to notice.

"Because you can read." Sister Auburn smiles. "Is that why Calder brought you here?"

I bite my lip and inhale deeply before answering so that bitterness doesn't taint my voice. "I think it is because I can paint."

"An artist." She claps her hands together and laughs. "We haven't had a new artist emerge in years. I tried to take some classes during my schooling days, but I definitely wasn't good at it. I can't wait for you to see the museum. You're going to love it. But I'm probably talking your ear off now. Let me show you back to your room. This is a lot to take in on your first day. It's better to learn these things slowly so that your brain has time to fully comprehend each new subject."

"Actually..." I pause at the door. "I'd like to take a look around the library if that's okay."

"Of course it's okay." Her smile doesn't fully reach her eyes as an inner conflict plays out behind them. "They'll start serving dinner in an hour though and the best foods get taken first."

"I won't be long," I reassure her. "I just want to take a look at these things called books."

*

"They said you were in here." Jillian's loud voice fills the quiet room.

But the room isn't really silent. Thousands of voices scream from pages tucked into every space of these massive shelves. Voices from the past, records, stories- all written down with letters. The handwriting is small, meticulous, almost inhuman. The letters drawn the same in so many books, but the voices are all different. Written in different ways, from different places, different authors and all from a world that doesn't exist anymore.

"Brooke, are you crying?" Jillian asks softly as she sets a plate of food down on the table next to me.

I angrily wipe a hand across my tired eyes. "It's so hard to read them."

"Don't worry about reading right now." She pulls out the chair beside mine. "They'll teach you to read over the next few months. Once you get the letters and sounds…"

"I know how to read." I slam the book shut. "But these aren't all real words."

"Hey now." She rubs my shoulder. "I'm not arguing that this place isn't awful. These people are delusional and this world shouldn't exist, but just because you don't know the words yet doesn't mean they don't exist."

"I don't want to speak their language," I spit through gritted teeth. "I want to go home."

Jillian pulls her hand back and drops it onto her lap as she stares blankly at the wall. "That's not going to happen. They'll never let us go back."

"We don't need their permission." I stand up, sending the chair crashing to the floor behind me. "I'll leave if I want to."

She leans her head back and closes her eyes. "Be careful talking about that kind of stuff here. There are eyes and ears everywhere. I wouldn't be surprised if they spy on us in our rooms."

My mind flashes with an image of Calder's paper- *it's called a map. That's what the textbook said-*

tucked behind the box closet. Panic makes my heart beat faster.

"What do you mean?" I gasp. "Why are they watching us?"

"Calm down." Her eyes open slowly. "They don't trust us until we earn our whites. Until then, they are making sure we don't run away or cause any problems."

"You don't seem to care about that," I huff. "Apparently all you do is cause problems."

"Aye," Jillian chuckles. "But not the danger to society kind of problems they are looking for."

"It's not like they can stop me if I want to leave." I fold my arms across my chest.

"Oh, they can," Jillian states. "And they will. Don't you think I already tried to run? Trust me, those safe padded rooms are not as comfortable as they sound."

The blood rushes from my face. "They locked you up?"

"For my own good," Jillian smirks. "But don't worry, that will never happen to you."

"You're right." I glare at the open door. "Because they are never going to catch me."

"No. That's not why." Jillian stands and places an arm over my shoulders, pulling my ear next to her lips. "It's because you are going to be a good girl and earn your whites."

*

Once I'm back in the room they gave me, I pull out the map and tuck it safely between the undergarments of the dress and my skin. I don't know if what Jillian says is true, but just to be safe I'll never let anyone find this.

The silence of the room punctuated by my shaky breaths does nothing to slow the racing of my thoughts. *I never should have helped Calder. I should have left when I got the chance.* Even thinking these things feels wrong. He would have died if I didn't save him.

But they say he saved me. Just the thought of that makes me laugh bitterly.

These words they use, all the words in the books, mean nothing. It's all nonsense. I don't want to learn them.

Except, a part of me does. I don't know why, but maybe if I can understand their words then I can find the right ones to use that will change things. They have to stop the retirement ships. They have to open the gates.

These people have no right to lie to us. All these sisters and mothers living on the land while my people suffer on the seas outside of the wall. *Mothers and sisters.* I roll my eyes. Those are some words that they don't understand.

If my sister knew what was happening... The image of Meghan's face brings hot tears to my eyes but I force myself to blink them away. A hollow, lonely ache fills my chest. I miss her so much. *I miss Zander and Thora and Rowan and Tordon and Lena so much already that it crushes my heart.* I promise myself I will see them again; Jillian's warning be damned. It may not be today, but I will find a way to go back.

For now, I need to find a way to fix this. I have to do it for Meghan. After all the times she spent shielding me from our mother's rage, it's my turn to protect her and her family from the lies these mothers tell.

Mothers. What a laughable notion. I know what it means to deal with an awful mother, and these women don't scare me. Their words don't scare me. I need to be strong enough to deal with this so I can find a way to make things right.

I curl into a ball on the soft bed, breathing steady to keep the homesick ache at bay. My eyes fixate on the gray sleeve of the dress I wear as the last of the fading daylight turns to the darkness of night.

White isn't even a color. It's the absence of colors. The color of color without color. My thoughts slow down as I drift off to sleep. Broken ideas become coherent truths. *Maybe Jillian is right. This dress needs to be white.*

☦ CHAPTER FOUR ☦

Living in someone else's world is exhausting. There's a constant tension in my neck as I try to move the way they do; try to speak the words they speak. All I want to do is scream at everyone and tell them I don't want to be here. I don't belong in this world. I want to go home.

*

Breakfast is a coagulated mess. Grains grown in fields, but not the wheat that makes the bread the watchmen served at their little village outside the marsh. This grain is clumpy and sticks to my spoon the same way it sticks to my tongue.

"You'll get used to the food." Jillian sighs as she sits down beside me. "Actually, you'll never get used to the taste, but your stomach won't hurt after a few weeks."

I silently nod and force myself to eat. There's no use in complaining. The other citizens-in-training all dressed in gray smile at one another as they enjoy their meal. Their smiles grow bigger still when a person wearing white takes notice of them or makes a kind remark. Like children eager for approval, they straighten their backs and balance their utensils delicately above the bowl.

"Why does everyone want to impress the mothers and sisters so badly?" I whisper to Jillian as I choke down another bite.

"They think it will help them earn their whites faster." She pushes her bowl away and leans her chin against her fist on the table.

"Will it?" I'm still not sure why this has to happen, but maybe if I can wear the clothes of these people then they might listen to my voice. If that is what it takes to fix this then I'm prepared to suffer through this game.

"No." Jillian gives me a mischievous smile. Her hand moves quickly, scooping up the bowl before I can register what is happening and slamming it down so that the gooey contents spread across the table. The noise echoes through the cafeteria so loudly that everyone turns to look at us.

"Stop it. What are you trying to do?" I whisper frantically. "We need to earn our whites."

There's a panic as Mother Wolfe and a man dressed in white come rushing through the large double doors.

"No, you need to earn your whites," Jillian mutters under her breath. "I'm helping you get them faster. Now go get something to clean this up."

My hesitation is cut short when Jillian screams, "Curse the gods, this food is garbage! If you aren't going to let us live in our homes then at least hire a decent cook."

I keep my eyes downcast and my head lowered as I rush to the servers' station. All the cooks glare at Jillian while they listen to her fit.

"May I have some rags?" I ask the server nearest me. He watches the scene over my shoulder, barely glancing my way as he throws a handful of torn cloth at my chest.

I have no clue what Jillian is up to and there isn't time to think. She slams her fists on the table.

"A bucket of fish bait is more appetizing than the crap you all are serving," she yells.

Mother Wolfe looks to me with pleading eyes as Jillian takes an aggressive step forward. I still don't know what I'm doing, but somehow the words come easily.

"Hey now, this isn't right." I reach out to Jillian to calm her down. "These people are our hosts. You know better than to act this way."

Jillian pushes her tongue in her cheek to hide her smile and turns so that Mother Wolfe can't see. Tremors shake her entire body. She looks exactly like Zander throwing a tantrum and it takes every ounce of willpower I have to not burst into laughter as I rub a soothing hand across her back.

"Why don't we clean this up?" I ask softly, handing her a rag. "Then we can talk to the staff and figure out a way to make the food more enjoyable for you."

"They won't listen," she grumbles.

"They might," I reassure her. "But we'll never know unless you can ask calmly and keep your anger in check."

Jillian hesitates, the pause is so dramatic, before reaching for the rag and sighing. She turns to the table and picks up the bowl. I help her clean the mess, glancing up to see Mother Wolfe watching with a beaming smile.

"It's a blessing you are here." She nods to me. I lower my eyes so she can't see the laughter within them.

"Come along, Benjamin." Mother Wolfe motions to the man beside her. "It seems we won't need your help after all. Our darling Brooke is perfectly capable of taking care of things."

*

"What was that?" I ask Jillian once they are out of earshot.

She flicks a sticky piece of grain from her finger, sending it flying across the table, and smiles. "You'll get your whites in no time at all."

*

The library doors sit propped open just as they were yesterday. The books I pulled from the shelves are still stacked upon the desk.

"Does no one use this room?" I ask Jillian as we walk past the one place I really want to be in this enormous dome.

"I suppose they do once they learn how to read." She shrugs and continues to walk down the hall like the room is nothing. "A few weeks ago, I saw some of the mothers coming here to study, but it's been empty since then."

"It's not that hard." I force myself to follow her. "I can teach you to read if you want."

"I've got most of it down. The letter sounds and all that. Sister Auburn is actually a good teacher," she smirks. "Now if only they could hire good cooks."

I roll my eyes. "If you know how to read, why don't you use the library?"

"Honestly?" She stares straight ahead. "I suppose I'm like the rest of them. The *why* doesn't bother me. I don't care about the history. But unlike the rest of those traitors all comfortable in their new home, I want to know how to fix it now."

Jillian's words weigh on me as we make our way to the classroom. I want to know everything. I want every truth of this world. There are so many lies I already know, but I do want to know the *why*.

Sister Auburn smiles warmly as we take our seats. She's pretty in a delicate way. The curve of her lips and the gleam in her eyes is so much like Calder's when he was happy. A happiness I only saw when we crossed the mountain pass. It's hard to blame him for that. He just wanted to come home. *I know that feeling all too well.*

"This is the perfect time for you to join us Brooke." Sister Auburn is practically bouncing out of her skin. "Today we are going over common terms for objects. Let's start with your rooms."

Her eyes scan the seats behind me and I turn to look. There are twelve people dressed in gray here in addition to me and Jillian. Eight of them are men, some with graying stubbles and some with bloody nicks on their chins. It makes shaving a beard seem dangerous. Four are women, but none my age. It dawns on me that I'm the youngest in the room.

"Now who remembers the terms we went over the last two weeks?" Sister Auburn asks.

An elderly man with a rounded belly and beard, still firmly attached to his chin, timidly raises his hand.

"Augusta," Sister Auburn states his name. "What can you remember?"

Augusta coughs to clear his throat. "The wardrobe holds clothes. The toilet is for waste. The sink is the washing basin. The sink, tub, and shower knobs run hot and cold water pumped through the dome's water heaters. The table, chairs, bedframe, and wardrobe are made from oak which is a type of wood. The plastic window shuts to prevent drafts and the screen keeps out bugs. The light switch turns on and off the electric lights that are powered by energy collected from the sun."

"Excellent," Sister Auburn beams and Augusta proudly smiles.

I didn't see a light switch in my room. My eyes dart around the classroom searching for whatever a light switch is.

"Don't worry, Brooke." Sister Auburn squats down in front of my desk. "These things take time to memorize. We'll go over them again. I don't want you to feel overwhelmed on your first day. This is just an introduction to the terms."

"I'm not overwhelmed." My brow furrows. "I remember everything he just said."

"Really?" she asks playfully. *She even speaks like her brother.*

"Yes." I stare back at her without blinking.

"Okay." She rocks back on her heels as she stands. "What's the name of the soft material on the floor?"

Augusta huffs behind me as if this game is already won. It might bother me if it wasn't such a ridiculous question.

"The material is comforting because it has meticulously woven fibers that cushion the foot, but I wouldn't exactly call it soft." I shrug. "You call it carpet."

Jillian snickers beside me as Sister Auburn's eyes widen in appreciation.

"Very good," she says. "You'll be caught up in no time at all."

*

"When do we learn the history of how this place came to be?" My fingers fidget anxiously with the material of my dress. I clasp my hands in front of me to keep them still. The rest of the class is taking a short break, walking around the halls and in the courtyard outside. I should have joined them. Sitting at a desk all morning is making me irritated.

"You are a wonder." Sister Auburn smiles warmly, tucking a stray piece of hair that escaped from the loose bun behind her ear. "Has anyone ever told you that?"

"Not really." My knee begins to bounce and I dig my foot into the floor to keep it steady. "I mean, people have wondered about me. But I'm not sure I've ever been called that specifically."

Sister Auburn giggles as she shakes her head. "Never mind. There aren't that many people that come here who actually care about the history of the world. They seem pretty content with their new and comfortable life. But then again, we don't get many younger people coming from outside the wall."

"Why is that?" I ask.

"Oh, I suppose it's because maturity and intelligence come with age," Sister Auburn sighs. "Plus, the older you are, the more versed you are in your craft." She misunderstood my question and it makes me instantly sick.

"I was wondering why they don't care about the history of the world," I explain, trying to keep my voice light despite the knot forming in my chest, "but now I'd like to know why you seem to value the elderly so much and still send retirement ships."

She looks horrified. I give her a gentle smile despite the bile rising in my throat. "I'm just curious is all."

"I don't know much about the retirement ships," she answers softly. "That's a part of the watchmen's job. The way it is explained is this is a mercy to the people. Old age isn't kind, especially when you have no real medical facilities or treatment. A final cruise filled with hope is better than years of suffering."

"But it's a lie." My fists clench at my side but I manage to keep my composure. Her face drops. She has no clue what she is saying. I wonder how many people living here even know about the ships.

Through the window, I see Augusta shuffling about the circular walkway in the court yard. His back is slightly hunched and he stops under the shade of a young tree to cough into his hand. *I bet she doesn't even know the real reason that younger people don't come here.* I can see it in the way that Augusta's eyes water as he stares at the peaceful valley view outside of the court yard. *The ones that are here don't have a reason to want to change anything.*

"If the people that come here from outside the walls are usually older, then why am I here?" I keep my voice as soft as I can, already knowing the answer.

"You must be very special," her face lights up as she compliments me. "They only bring the people who don't deserve that kind of life."

No, it's not! I want to scream. *It's because they didn't consider me a threat. They thought I wouldn't fight.*

I stand up from my desk, smoothing the wrinkles from my dress, and give her a modest smile.

"I'm not so sure how special I am, but I'd really like to learn the history of how this world came to be."

*

"Take as much time as you need," Sister Auburn says as she pulls two more books from the shelves. "This stack you started with is a little too advanced..." Her voice trails off as my eyes dart to her face.

"They aren't the right kind of books," she hurries to explain. "I have to go back and start the reading lessons with the class, but I'll be in the building until around dinnertime, so come find me if you have any questions."

There's a textbook held together by metal rings with a faded image of children playing in the grass on the cover. My fingerprints leave smudges on the plastic that thickly coats each page. The words are easier to pronounce, but the stories in the book are hard to read.

A whole section dates a timeline of history before the rising seas. Next are notes called geography describing the entire continent of North America. *Or what used to be the continent.* A plastic overlay lifts up allowing me to see what was before. I don't need to pull out Calder's map to know that the lines here before me are the same. I already have it memorized.

My finger trails up the mountain ridge that used to be called The Rockies. These mountains are all that remain of the ancient world. I knew there was land right under our feet on the sea, but I could never have imagined there was this much of it.

And what became of the rest of the earth? This can't be all there is. I quickly pull up the book labeled *World History* and scan the pages. There are mountain ranges on many continents, but no plastic overlay to show me what is left. I place *World History* to the side for now and dig deeper into the contents that describe how this world used to be.

Pain. *How could the people that lived before us go through all this pain?* There was so much fighting. Wars after wars, destruction, plagues, money- they were fighting over so many things. All that land was there for them and they took it for granted. Farms full of food as big as the land mass I stand on, things they call rainforests and deserts. They could even travel through the skies and to the stars. By gods, they had everything. *How could they not see it?*

Traveling by sea became a luxury in ancient times. Expensive homes and bustling cities lined the coastal areas. I wonder if these people would want to live there now? When being on the ocean means you are cast out from the earth, clinging to the rusted metal wall like sea barnacles.

I quickly skim through the books Sister Auburn left out. Most of these stories of the past I already know. The old ones pass them down in songs and elaborately spun tales, but the truth is still the same if I compare them to the written word.

What I want to know is less distant in history, after the core of the planet heated causing the seas to rise and the earth to shift. She didn't put any books like this on the stack.

I stretch my neck from side to side to relieve some of the tension from reading for so long as I search through the books still on the shelves. I have to find them. There needs to be documentation of the madness that is our world.

A row of leatherbound books on the far wall catches my eye. I pull out the first one to inspect. *Records of the Mother, Volume I.* The text is handwritten, its words curving and almost illegible compared to the words printed from typing machines or printing presses in the ancient world as the textbook explained. The entire row on the shelf is filled with volumes labeled and numbered like this, but I know enough to realize I'd better start at the beginning.

☦ CHAPTER FIVE ☦

After the violence and bloodshed, one mother said enough. Her name is insignificant, as she wished it to be, for she was all of us. She spoke for every mother protecting every child that would ever be born on the earth.

The mother bent the ear of violent men and forced them to lay down their weapons. In her homespun dress of faded cotton and crown of wildflowers on her head, she stood toe to toe with the strongest warrior. A gentle touch was all it took to steady his hand.

Following her lead, more mothers stepped from their destroyed homes with small babes in arms. They stood tall beside her, demanding an end to the bloodshed.

May we always remember the courage of the mother.

Meghan's image swirls with the story in my mind. I can see her standing on the docks with a crown made of rusted iron and bent coral adorned with pearls set upon her head while she holds Zander on her hip and threatens the fishermen to behave. The thought of it makes me laugh.

The mothers' voices were clear and loud. A wall was to be built. This was the only way to protect the earth. Angry men had fought too long over the precious few resources of the land. The mother stood in a recently burnt forest, ashes cooling near her bare feet, condemning the beasts for yet another petty altercation.

With shame in their eyes, the men agreed and turned their weapons factory into a production house to build the wall. Forty-feet high with guarded entrance ways at the seven most accessible points, the wall was built to withstand the rising seas.

And those who could not live peacefully were banished from the earth.

My eyes quickly scan the text, but there are only pages of construction details. It took them thirty years to complete. There was a lot of prosperity during this time. Everything seemed to be going well for these *mothers…*

Records of the Mother, Volume II.

The mother has aged. She now walks slowly, her children have grown and made lives for themselves in this peaceful world. Trouble makers are displaced from the earth, sent out beyond the walls. City builders and welders now unemployed have been assigned to construct wharves to serve as functioning landscape on the seas outside the gates.

The aged mother personally oversees this planning, hoping every person, no matter their disposition, lives a life that benefits them in some way.

One night during this building phase, a young soldier, disgruntled at being sent outside the wall, sneaks back in through the open gates and slits the mother's throat while she sleeps.

A great mourning sweeps the nation. The daughters of the mother join with their common sisters, now all mothers themselves, and demand the gates be sealed. The mother's sons step forward to volunteer as the first watchmen.

I shove the book away and lean my forehead against the aged wooden desk. The curves of the wood indent in my skin and I push harder against it, willing the desk itself to explain to me how the hell this all is happening. This was hundreds of years ago and there are still ten more volumes to get through.

Is this hatred for what happened to one woman so ingrained in their stories that they can't separate themselves from it? But I feel it too. Reading these words makes me feel awful for the brave woman who stood up for her children so long ago.

Maybe she was right to send the trouble makers outside the wall, but I didn't do anything wrong. I was born there, just like my father and grandmother and great-grandmother. Generations before me were all born on the sea. And if we cause problems, our life is over. There's no where else to push the trouble makers away, I guess. *But what did I do to make my life worth less than the people here?*

I skip over Volume III and carry Volume IV back to the table. They all seem to say the same thing, I'm hoping this one will explain more.

The granddaughters of the original mother, and we are all her granddaughters, sit on the High Council. Gone are the barbaric ways of men.

Peace and prosperity fill the land. All men between the ages of sixteen and twenty-four must serve on the watch. Their aggression and strength are better served outside the wall.

What kind of a mother forces her own son away? The irony of all this is too much. The paper crinkles as I flip through the pages, skimming details of how easy they made life on the land, until the word "rebellion" catches my eye.

Word of rebellion has begun to spread. More and more attacks on watchmen are reported to the council. The growing unrest is addressed in the quarterly scheduled meeting. High Mother Ustus makes the following declaration:

> *"The people who live outside the walls have fallen too far from civilization. There is no culture, no betterment of society. They are truly barbaric.*
>
> *Whether it is the seed of the first trouble makers, laced with anger and destruction in their DNA, that continued to repopulate, or if it is due to the rough nature of their circumstances, it matters not. These people will destroy the earth if given the chance.*
>
> *But I will not condone violence with further violence. Instead, I will give them hope. Something they do not have. The watchmen's reports on the sick and elderly are too inhumane to repeat in this room. Just know they receive little to no care, rotting away in suffering like wild animals. I propose we afford a reprieve at the age of sixty. If they can behave, they will be given passage away from their terrible existence. It will be a mercy to them, as the original mother would have wanted."*

"Are you able to understand those?" Sister Auburn's voice breaks my concentration on the text. I force myself to blink, to hide the burning rage in my eyes, before looking up at her.

"Most of it," I answer softly.

"That's wonderful." She smiles as I close the book. "What volume are you on now? Number four? Can you believe that was written almost three hundred years ago? The word choice is a little strange and you'll have to excuse that dark time in our history."

"Have things changed much since then?" My tone is as dry as my throat is. If she caught the double edge to my question, she skillfully ignores it.

"By leaps and bounds," Sister Auburn laughs. "There once was a time when my brother and I wouldn't have been allowed in the same classroom. Thank goodness for change, right?"

I lower my head and say nothing, which is better than letting the wave of my honest thoughts spill out into the dome.

"Hey." She reaches out and pats my hand gently. "I can't imagine how hard this is for you. There's so much you don't know. I wish they had some type of education outside the wall, but you are amazing. Even without a classroom, you still learned how to read and now you are devouring a century worth of history in a few hours. Take it slower though, there's a reason we don't go over everything in one day. Learning new things can be overwhelming."

I resist the urge to smack her hand away and force my lips into a tired smile. "Why do you think we aren't given an education?"

The insult that she doesn't think is an insult sits on the tip of her tongue, but she doesn't say it aloud. Instead, she shrugs and smiles. "It's probably because survival takes a lot of time. There's not much left of the day for learning."

She thinks we are all barbarians. Things haven't changed much in three hundred years. "Maybe." I nod.

"I have a surprise for you," she quickly changes the subject. "Tomorrow after class I'm going to take you to the art museum so you can see all the famous paintings."

"What?" My breath quickens in excitement despite the deep-rooted anger in the pit of my stomach. It's like I have no control over this physical reaction. *There are others here who love to paint,* the thought makes me feel lightheaded. *Other people just like me.*

I want to know what they've created. I want to meet them and hear them talk. The selfish part of me needs to see this with my own eyes even as my family suffers behind their wall. I just want to know what they do, how they think. That's not too much of a betrayal. *Is it?*

"I hope this means you are happy." She takes a step back to study my face.

My eyes well with tears. I can speak truth even if this world cannot. "Yes. I would be so happy to see them."

*

Jillian catches me in the hall just as Sister Auburn waves goodbye.

"She's taken a liking to you," Jillian whispers in my ear even though Sister Auburn is almost to the exit and the two of us walk alone heading deeper into the dome.

"Why would she do that?" I lower my own voice in response. The tone comes naturally to me, it's how we'd always spoken on the wharf when we weren't sure if the watchmen were nearby. But here in these empty halls my voice seems to echo so that every single plank of wood can hear it.

"Probably because you are smart," Jillian chuckles, almost bitterly. "I guess I always knew that, but seeing a Sister take so much interest in you is a little weird."

"I can make it stop." I'm joking, but a part of me is worried. If I upset Sister Auburn, I may never meet the painters or see Calder again.

"Don't do that," Jillian whispers harshly. "If she likes you then this will help your case. The goal is to earn your whites. She can help with that."

We reach the room numbered 14, *my room*, and Jillian walks inside.

"I still don't understand what the plan is." I close the door behind me. "How will earning a white pair of clothes fix anything for our families?"

"You're not stupid." Jillian sighs as she falls down on my bed. "Don't pretend to be."

"They're not going to listen to me." I unlace the constricting shoes they give us, leaving them by the door, before padding barefoot across the comforting carpet. Jillian moves her legs over as if annoyed at the inconvenience, allowing me room to sit.

"I've read their history books. These people have no respect for those who live outside the wall." The edge of the bed is the only place I fit now. She takes the rest of the space.

"But you're not outside the wall anymore." She crosses her arms behind her head and arches an eyebrow. "And you are a woman. Have you noticed how they treat men here? If Augusta or that nice man Peter or any of the other dried up sea urchins acted the way I do then they'd be thrown back out into the ocean."

Jillian pauses, seeing the gears turning in my brain. "They'd be tossed out dead, Brooke. Don't get your hopes up."

My hope deflates just as quickly as it came. "It's their history books. They seem to think that violence is a male problem."

Jillian snorts through her nose. "I wonder what they think of me then."

"Probably that you are broken." I wink. "Why do they keep you around anyway?"

"It was my mother's fault," she sighs. "She should have been able to teach them the aquaponics system better."

"Is Vera still here?" I venture to ask.

"No." Jillian's face hardens. "I'll explain it to you tomorrow after class. You can come to work with me in the afternoon."

"I can't tomorrow." My eyes lower, studying the intricate pattern of the twisted fibers that make up the carpet. "Sister Auburn is taking me somewhere."

"That's good." Jillian suddenly sits up straight, swinging her legs off the bed. "You should make friends with her. Just remember not to trust these people. They're all brainwashed, we can't help them, but we need to find a way to save our people."

*

The morning sun filters through the plastic windowpane. I've been watching the light move through the room for the past hour. Little dust particles swirl around in the rays. They are the only thing that seems to moving right now. It's too early to be awake in this world. I wish the day would hurry up and start.

Warm water fills the tub and I sink gently into it. There are various jars of soap on the shelf near the knobs that smell like the flowers which lined the path that brought me here. I pick up the purple tinted one and sniff it. The scent mixing with the rising steam of the water is so overwhelming that it makes me gag.

Hastily, I pull the plug. The warm water swirls as it rushes down the pipes. The frigid blast from the knob labeled "cold" sends shivers down my spine. I sit under the stream with my eyes closed, pretending I am home.

My hand lingers on my father's jacket hanging in the wardrobe. It's dry now. The two clean gray dresses are the same, made from the same soft cloth with the same dull shape. Still, I hold them both up to the light trying to see which one looks best. *It's a tie.*

I walk slowly, oh so slowly, to the cafeteria. No one is here besides the servers and chefs who are only now beginning to set up. The same man who tossed me the rags yesterday now gives me his full attention accompanied by an anxious smile.

"I'm sorry, ma'am," he says to me. "Food will be ready in a few minutes."

"Oh, it's alright." I nod politely. "I'll just sit here and wait."

My body stays perfectly motionless as I watch the world waking outside the windows of the cafeteria, but my heart beats so frantically inside of my chest that it feels like it's going to explode. *Move faster,* I want to scream. But even my lips stay still.

"The early bird gets the worm." The male server smiles as he sets a plate of steaming eggs and meat on the table beside me. From his apron pocket he produces a glass jar filled with white crystals.

My eyes widen at the sight of it. "Salt?"

He laughs at the surprise on my face. "You can give some to your friend too, as long as you keep her quiet."

"Of course." I smile gratefully. "What's your name?"

"Mercury." He tips an invisible hat. "Pleasure to meet you."

"And you." I nod.

"Do you need anything else?" He glances over his shoulder as Augusta comes shuffling into the cafeteria and heads to the serving station.

"Um." I bite my lip, torn between the thought of feeling stupid and the driving need to know more. "Just one thing, if you don't mind. Can you tell me why the early bird gets the worm?"

*

The morning class is as stagnant as boat sails on a rare day with no wind. I have to physically force myself to keep my feet from tapping against the stone floor. *Tile, they call it tile.*

Jillian was pleased with the salt. She sits a little straighter in her seat today. Sister Auburn gushes like a proud parent every time I answer a question correctly. The class is discussing etiquette. *Fridays are for etiquette.* Plates and forks and spoons- they all seem to have a very special position here in this world. It seems ridiculous, but from the corner of my eye I see the rest of the class hanging on every word like it's a knowledge they can't wait to scoop up with a right placed, after the knife, spoon.

"Your clothes are just as important as your manners," Sister Auburn explains. "A healthy citizen does not wear dirty or stained clothes. You'll understand this more when you get your whites. We work hard to keep ourselves clean and presentable, and for now you can practice on your grays." She continues with a lesson about handwashing and cleanliness, like we don't know how to bathe. My fingers tap against the desk and I press them down so they lay still.

I stay seated through the lecture on letters. They repeat *ch, sh, br, tr* sounds. My gaze drifts to the open window. Little brown birds hop along the sweeping branches of the tree they call a willow. Its leaves are curled, winter burnt, and ready to drop to the ground. Supposedly in spring they'll be bright green. *Bright green is algae growing on the rocks and coral on the ocean floor.*

I've aged a hundred years by the time Sister Auburn finally announces the end of class.

*

"Are you ready?" Sister Auburn asks as the other citizens-in-training leave for whatever work occupies their afternoons. Jillian gives me a long and pointed look before exiting the room.

Relief washes over me as I stand and nod. I don't want to seem nervous or overly excited, so I remain silent. Sister Auburn radiates enough excitement for the two of us anyway.

"Let's go," she laughs as she pulls me by the arm.

The roads are paved and lined with walkways called sidewalks on either side. Carts propelled by bicycles amble up and down the center of the road. Everyone seems to smile with perfectly shaped teeth, waving at one another as they pass.

There's so much room here to walk that it makes me feel smaller than I really am. Sister Auburn, who is just my size, takes no notice of this feeling. She walks briskly, the cool winds that drift over the fields of brown grass tease at her hair. When her forehead isn't creased in thought she is really pretty. I tug at the gray sleeves of my dress wishing I didn't feel so out of place and uncomfortable in my own skin.

We pass a row of tables outside of a small tavern. *Not a tavern, a restaurant.* The tables are clear with glass bottles holding muted colors of dried flower bouquets. A group of young women all wearing white look up at me curiously over the delicate cups they hold in their hands.

"Just this way." Sister Auburn guides me across the street toward another dome. This building is a little smaller than the Welcome Center and the sign out front reads "District Fine Arts Museum." My palms begin to sweat despite the even cooler breeze that greets us once the doors open.

"It's a little chilly in here," she apologizes as the doors close behind us. "Most of the collections of art are very old and they do their best to control the climate in order to preserve them."

Hearing this deflates my anxiety and everything else along with it. "I thought we were going somewhere where people paint."

"Like a workshop?" Her forehead creases. "They might have events like that. I do know a few professors at the university that will definitely want to meet you and they have classes there."

My lips form a tight line as I study the mosaic pattern on the floor. I didn't realize just how much this meant to me until it was gone. "Oh," is all I manage to say.

"Oh Brooke!" She rushes to my side. "I didn't mean to give you the wrong impression. This is my fault. You're so quick to pick up on everything that it's easy to forget I have to be careful with my words."

I don't want her sympathy. "It's alright." My eyes meet hers and I smile. "A museum is a place to showcase things such as paintings. I'd really love to see them."

☦ CHAPTER SIX ☦

I wasn't prepared for this.

Paintings lay inside plastic cases an arm deep and out of reach. A trick of the light allows you to see them, but they are so far away it's like reaching to the bottom of the ocean to try and grasp a bright red piece of coral. It takes a few minutes until I can adjust to the light and shock of not being allowed to touch them.

Some aren't even paintings at all. There are no raised edges, just a flat replica of a scene like someone took an exact image from their eyes and placed it on paper. Sister Auburn lingers at each display, but I can't do that.

An urgent need to see everything all at once consumes me. Halls after halls are filled with various cases and there is no one here but the two of us to admire them. My breathing becomes more shallow at each passing canvas.

Colors and textures swirl into blurred images in my mind. A hand, a cloth blowing in the breeze, the eyes of a man so hollow that I want to rip my heart out and lay it at his feet just so he can feel again.

"What do you think?" Sister Auburn is suddenly beside me in the dark recesses of the dome where I stare at the celebration of Tripp Ainsworth.

On center display is a painting titled "Midnight Nights," where a naked, dark gray skinned woman with pointed ears and fiery red hair lounges on a brightly colored bed.

"I could never be this good." The words fall from my mouth honestly.

"Nonsense." She shakes her head, unwilling to hear the truth. "They wouldn't have saved you if you weren't this good. My brother wouldn't have…" Her voice trails off. There are other truths she is hiding.

"Wouldn't have?" I urge her to continue.

"Never mind." She smiles brightly. "That's for him to discuss. But I'll bet you have loads of talent just waiting to be tapped into. Which paintings did you think were awful?"

Her question makes me laugh. "They are all good, Sister Auburn."

"You can call me Charlotte." Her smile falters, but she regains it defiantly. "Anywhere but the classroom, you can call me Charlotte. Now tell the truth, which one didn't you like?"

My eyes dart around the room, but this section is full of talent. "There were a few weird ones down the hall. All straight lines and flat color. I think I could paint better than those."

"There you have it!" Charlotte exclaims as she laces her arm through mine. "You are already more talented than some of the greatest artists in the past 700 years. Give it a week or two and you'll be ranked among the best."

Her enthusiasm is contagious. I want to bottle it up. "When can I meet the other painters you speak of?"

"I think soon." We stroll arm in arm through the halls filled with the expressions of dead artists. "You're already my star pupil. I'm sure you'll earn your whites in no time at all."

*

We walk deeper into the city where the cluster of smaller domes blocks out the view of the fields. Shops with windows display their wares hidden beneath the glass like the paintings in their tombs. This is nothing like the main wharf in my city. No one calls out prices, no shop owners stand guarding their products from wandering hands. There is a steady stream of foot traffic, but it all just seems too quiet as people politely step out of each other's way.

I keep my head down as I walk. The curious glances quickly thrown in my direction make it seem as if I'm being watched. *Everyone is watching me.* I try my hardest to keep my steps deliberate and light.

"Over here." Charlotte tugs on my arm, pulling me inside the bakery she insisted that we stop at. The warm smell of baking bread fills my nose. This is one of the smells that I've already grown to like, there is something comforting about it.

"They have the best almond croissants," she explains as she places an order at the counter. I smile and nod like I've understood everything she's just said. *I'm getting too good at this.*

The pastry flakes into pieces as I bite the soft dough. "You're right," I say, savoring the invigorating taste of brown sugar and cinnamon that coats my tongue. "This is amazing."

"See," she laughs after swallowing another bite, "I knew you'd like them. They are Calder's favorite too."

This information feels wrong to me, like I'm taking secret pieces from his life that he wouldn't want anyone to know. Except, she gives it away so innocently that I can't help but smile.

"I can't imagine him ever being in a place like this." I sweep the almond slivers- *almonds are nuts-* that fell on the table into my hand and put them back on the plate. "Or any watchmen for that matter."

"That's why they serve on the watch," Charlotte sighs. "It isn't their fault, it's just biology. Men are a little too aggressive during their teenage years. Calder is different though."

"Is he?" I arch an eyebrow and laugh. "He seems to fit in with the rest of the watchmen just fine."

"And he should," she explains. "He has a job to do after all, but I don't think he's the type to cause problems. He's too playful, too nice, and he thinks too much."

It's hard to reconcile the Calder Charlotte speaks of and the Calder I know. Maybe I got a small glimpse of it on this side of the mountain, but it was over too soon to be able to really understand him.

"I hope he wakes up soon," I whisper.

"Me too." She reaches across the table and gives my hand a gentle squeeze. The touch is comforting, something Meghan would have done. *I actually want to like Charlotte.* The realization takes me by surprise.

"Should we go back to the Welcome Center now?" I pull my hand to my lap.

"If you want." She shrugs. "Everyone is off tomorrow and I have nothing to do tonight. I can show you around the city if you like."

"That would be nice." I really mean this. "But I'm exhausted. That was a lot to take in today."

"See! I told you it's best to take in new things slow," she laughs. "Let's get you back home and we'll take a tour another day."

We walk down a different sidewalk on a different street. This one has less traffic. Up on the hill is a field filled with children all laughing and rolling in the grass. At first it seems that their white clothes are dirty and I wonder how their mothers will ever get them clean, but then I realize they wear the same shade of gray that I do. Heat rushes to my cheeks and I look quickly away. Charlotte, *Sister Auburn,* continues walking, oblivious to my reaction.

Their children wear gray because they haven't yet earned their whites. This is what the council thinks of us. We are nothing but ignorant children from outside the wall who they've graciously decided to adopt. *Do they pity us like children too?* I think of Zander and all the words I've used to placate him, to make him follow the rules. The little trinkets, extra time spent with him…

Oh gods, this is embarrassing. No wonder the people of this world eyed me curiously in the street. They must see me as a grown child. That's all I am to them. A hard knot forms in my stomach as I walk. *I am not weak. I am not ignorant. Maybe I once was, but that time has passed.*

"Are you alright?" Sister Auburn stops and waits for me. I hurry to catch up.

"Of course, Charlotte." I wrap my arm through hers and force a smile. "Why wouldn't I be?"

The laughter of the children catches her attention and the color drains from her face. "Listen,

I'm serious. You will get your whites soon. There's no need for you to be at the Welcome Center much longer. You don't belong there."

"Whatever you and the Mothers think is best." It takes everything in me to keep my voice soft, compliant.

Sister Auburn pulls me closer to her side. "I'm so happy you are here."

*

It's dark but not true black. Deep blues and heavy greens surround me, sucking me into the abyss that allows no light. A swirling cloud of this darkness is all I can see.

A white flash as quick as a lightning bolt temporarily blinds me. I panic. My heart pounds against my chest. I don't know which way to go. When the lightning comes back again, this time with teeth- pearly white teeth- that snap through the blinding darkness, primeval fear takes over.

I need to swim. Up through the darkness, as fast as I can. *Oh gods, I hope this way is up.* If I don't move, I'm going to die. There's light that way. Lighter hues of blues and greens. I jump, breaking the surface. Something hard and dry catches my fall.

It's too bright now. Yellows and oranges and the brightest blue I've ever seen. *I can't breathe!* My back arches unnaturally as I try to suck in air.

Everything is too dry. My skin is ripping against the hard surface. I kick out my legs and arms, but I can't make myself move. In a panic, I twist my body any way I can, willing myself back into the darkness. Whatever the white lightning is, it can't be worse than this…

*

"Brooke!" A happy voice breaks through the blinding light and pulls me from the depths of the nightmare. I gulp in air in painful gasps, grateful to be able to breathe again.

"Brooke, wake up." The sound of knocking fills Room 14. *My room*. The room they gave me. The voice is giddy and song-like. I can't seem to place it.

"Come on Brooke, you need to get up. It's me Rosemary."

Early dawn grayish light filters weakly through the window blinds. I wrap the blanket around my body and force my feet to the floor, leaving the warmth of the bed behind me, and open the door before she has the chance to knock again.

"What's happening?" The electric light of the hallway temporarily blinds me and I shudder as I remember the nightmare. "Is everything okay?"

Rosemary's smile spreads across her face. "Better than okay. Calder is awake."

*

A layer of frost covers the brown grass that lines the sidewalk. I shiver under the thin dress wishing I would have grabbed my father's jacket. These people take their clothes so seriously though, I don't know if wearing the tanned leather coat would offend them. Rosemary is practically skipping ahead of me.

"He was calling out for you in his sleep all night," she turns and whispers conspiratorially. "Then when he woke up, your name was the first word on his lips."

Hearing this sends an embarrassing wave of heat coursing through my body that combats the chill of the early morning. I wrap my arms around my chest and hurry to catch up. *He's probably just worried I ran away.*

The hospital is quiet and dimly lit. Our footsteps seem out of place as they echo through the halls. Rosemary takes me to the same room he was in the morning I left him here.

"Go in." She nudges me forward to the open door, leaving me alone with a playful wink.

As I step inside, the curtain is pulled back. A woman in a long coat holding a clipboard- *a doctor-* looks up startled to see me standing here.

"Ah, you must be Brooke," she says as the shock fades. "You don't look so well. Are you sick?"

"No." I shake my head. "Just tired."

"Do you not sleep well?" She takes a step forward, studying my face. I step to the side, giving room for her to pass and hoping she will leave.

When she doesn't budge, I let out a sigh. "I have silly nightmares sometimes."

"Nightmares?" Her face is full of concern. "Did they start when you got here?"

I lower my eyes, wishing she'd stop staring at me so intently. "I've had them my whole life."

"I see." She chews the end of her pen before finally looking away. "Why don't we set you up with an appointment and I'll see what I can do to help you make them stop? Nightmares are not common here, but there are ways to fix them. You shouldn't have to live like that."

"No thank you." I ignore her stunned expression. "I already know how to handle them."

"And how is that?" She watches me curiously. Calder coughs from behind the curtain and relief floods through me.

"They go away if I work hard through the day or when I get a chance to paint. Now if you'll excuse me, can I go see him?"

"Of course." She hesitates by the door. "But promise to come see me if you ever want the help."

My reassuring nod is full of lies, but it satisfies her enough to make her leave. My heart suddenly begins to beat faster as I turn to face the curtain. For some reason, I can't force my feet to move. My hands twist themselves around each other as I try to think of what I want to say.

"I thought you were coming to see me," Calder's deep voice calls out. It sounds strong and steady. I can hear the laughter within his words. The tension eases from my shoulders and I smile in spite of myself.

"Nightmares?" he asks as I step around the curtain. If his bandaged head wasn't cocked to the side with a goofy grin plastered across his face, I'd be tempted to throw something at him.

"You're in a lot of them," I smirk.

"That's the way you talk to an injured man?" He places a hand over his heart as if I'd stabbed him there.

"That's the way I talk to an injured, stupid watchman who I dragged on a stretcher through the middle of the night for five miles on a road that I had no clue where it went and into a crazy new world that I don't understand." The words rush from my lips untethered. It's freeing to speak them out loud. Relief and anger mix together, making me happy that I can finally speak this truth. *So why do I feel sad when the smile drops from his face?*

"Thank you," he says solemnly. "Thank you for saving my life."

My sarcastic response dies on my tongue. Maybe I shouldn't be so harsh. "How are you feeling?"

His eyes light up as the smile returns. "Honestly? A little ridiculous and I've got this killer headache for some reason."

"I'm surprised a rock could damage that thick skull of yours," I laugh, moving closer to the bed.

"I swear that pool used to be deeper," he sighs.

"It's probably the same size, you just got bigger." My words hang in the air, the unspoken meaning drifting between the two of us. I'm sad for him. He lost his home and the rest of his youth just because of his *biology*. I wonder if he feels this way or if he is brainwashed like the rest of them.

"You don't look good in gray," he finally says, breaking the tension.

"Well lucky for me, I should be getting my whites soon." I roll my eyes. "Or at least that's what your sister says."

"My sister?" His jaw drops. "You've already met Charlotte?"

"And your mother." I glare at him. "Maybe you should have warned me about what I was walking in to."

"Charlotte is the teacher in the family, not me. How was I supposed to word this all in a way you would understand?" He leans back against the pillows. "Was my mother upset?"

"You haven't seen her?"

"No." He gives me a sheepish smile full of other things I don't understand. "I just woke up."

"Then why am I here?" I chew my lip, studying his response.

"I wanted to make sure you were okay," he states as a matter of fact.

"I could have run." I cross my arms.

"You could have, but you didn't." He nods and the motion sends a wave of pain across his face. His lips pinch together turning purple as he shuts his eyes tight. Worry forces me to his side.

"Are you okay?" I ask grabbing his hand. It's warm and calloused, just like I remember when he led me blind to the river. He closes his fingers, completely engulfing my hand within his. When I look back up, he is staring at me. His dark brown eyes glistening with moisture, tears of pain, but he doesn't cry.

He licks his dry lips and inhales deeply. "I think I like holding your hand."

"What type of medicine do they have you on?" I giggle nervously, but don't pull away.

"I don't know." He closes his eyes. "Whatever it is, it's good."

Calder drifts in and out of sleep. There's no use having a conversation, but when I try to leave his hand tightens holding me by his side. I stay until his breathing becomes even, watching his chest rise and fall. It's comforting in a way I can't describe. It almost feels like home.

But that's not true. He isn't home. He's as far away from home as I am now, as this entire world is. Yet I can still clearly picture his face drenched in seawater after he dove into the ocean after Zander and me. His fingers strumming against the guitar in the tavern. His body leaning against the rocks on the short beach exposed by low tide under my father's machine…

Stupid, stupid, stupid. I feel so unbelievably stupid. Everything I gave up to learn these truths. I gave up my entire life. And for what? These lies are hundreds of years in the making. Nothing is ever going to change. *No. I can find a way to fix this.* I have to find a way to change things.

Calder hasn't stirred in a while. His fingers loosen their grip. I watch his face. With his jaw relaxed he looks so childlike and peaceful. As quietly as I can, I remove my hand from under his and stand up from the edge of the hospital bed.

"Brooke," he calls out drowsily. I pause mid-step. "Will you come back to see me soon?"

I can't say no. How can I say no? I turn to look but his eyes are still closed. His mind stuck somewhere between the dream world and this one.

"Of course I will," I answer gently. He smiles in his sleep and I leave the room listening to the sounds of his steady breathing once more.

*

"How is he?" Rosemary meets me at the hospital exit. Her enthusiasm from the morning escapade has faded, now she yawns as she leans against the wall.

"He's sleeping again. What did you give him that makes him act drunk?" The warm sun is already melting the frost on the grass outside.

"Nothing really." She falls into step beside me. "He refused pain medications and antibiotics don't generally make people loopy."

"Antibiotics?" *Another word I need to look up.*

"I can't believe they don't have antibiotics outside the wall." Her mouth opens wide. I wonder if a bug will fly into it. "What do they give you when you get an infection?"

Infection is like rot. "We pray to the gods." I meant it as a joke, but it didn't come out that way.

Tears of pity form in her eyes. "I'm so sorry you had to live like that."

"Don't be." I hug my arms to my chest and silently walk back to the Welcome Center. Rosemary stays with me and I'm not sure why. I know which way to go. I'm just about to ask her what she is doing when she pauses at the crosswalk.

"I've got to get some sleep now, but if you are free this evening, do you want to come hang out with me and some friends?" she asks hopefully. It catches me off guard. I look to her white clothes, the shirt hem catching in the morning breeze, and then down to my own gray dress.

"Why?" It's more of a statement than a question, but she eagerly fills the quiet between us.

"It'll be good for you to get out of that stuffy old dome and have some fun. I promise not all of us are as boring as the Mothers."

I bite my lip to hide my smile. That's not what I was expecting to hear. "I'd like that." At least I think I would. I'm not sure what I'd like anymore. Calder's smile and the way he grabbed my hand teases me, making me question reality. *Actually, this whole place has me questioning everything about reality.*

"Perfect." Rosemary claps her hands together. "I'll come pick you up before dinner."

She races away across the road despite the lack of busy traffic. The city is just now lazily waking despite the sun being firmly in the sky. The people move slow, still smiling and waving to one another. I linger at the intersection and watch them.

It's nothing like the way things work in my city. By this time of day there'd be much less commotion on the wharf, but that's only because the throngs of fishermen would be gone right now, working on a cluster of boats out on the sea. Even on a weekend like today, the shops would have already been open and the venders trading goods might have sold out hours ago. It's like these people just rolled out of bed with nothing to do but smile.

A frown pulls down my lips as I study the scene. I, too, have nothing to do today until I meet with Rosemary. It's a surreal feeling that makes my heart flip inside my rib cage and causes me to panic. *I think I'll go to the library. There's a lot left to learn.*

*

"You missed breakfast," Jillian tells me as she strolls through the open doors and leans against the table that I've covered with books. The Mother's volumes are boring me now. Two hundred years without an incident. It seems everyone learned their place.

"I know." I rub my fists against my eyes and lean back in the chair. "When is lunch?"

"In about an hour." Her eyebrows pinch together as she watches me. "I've been looking for you all morning. I guess I should have known you'd be here."

"The dome isn't really that big," I laugh. "Where did you think I was?"

Jillian shifts uncomfortably as she looks to the books still nestled on the shelves against the wall. "Well, I wasn't looking for you all morning exactly. Peter met me in the hall and asked if I wanted to take a walk."

It takes me a moment to place the name. Peter is the quiet man with the thick black beard dotted with silver who sits in the back of the class. His muscles stretch the men's gray shirt as he leans on his elbows, struggling to memorize the world terms.

"Why did Peter want to walk with you?" I can't help the teasing of my voice. She's obviously embarrassed by the question, but I think it's in a good way.

"That's none of your business." Her lips are tight, hiding a smile behind them.

"If it wasn't my business, then you shouldn't have brought it up." *Gods it is funny to watch her squirm.*

"Never mind this now," she snaps. "Are you reading anything in here that will help our people?"

"No." I close the book I'm holding and push the rest away to clear room on the desk for my forehead. "These people are delusional and I don't know that anything will change their minds. They think they've created the perfect society and we are just savage animals living outside the wall."

She chews on these words for a minute before leaning down to whisper in my ear, "We could try showing them what animals are really like."

"No." My eyes dart to the last volume of the mothers dated thirty years ago. "There has to be a way to change things without fighting. The watchmen would slaughter our people with their weapons. We have to find a way to change things peacefully."

"Alright." Jillian slumps into the chair beside me. "It was just a thought. We still need to get you your whites so you stand a chance at speaking to them and actually having them listen. I'm trying to think of our next move, something to get them to truly accept you as one of their citizens." Her whisper fades to silence as she looks over her shoulder at the empty library.

"I'm going out with Rosemary tonight," I state with a smile on my face. "She's very sweet and works at the hospital. I'm excited to meet more people here."

Jillian nods, understanding my meaning without the explanation. "Okay." But the word seems bitter. I can't tell if she's acting or not. "Just remember where you came from."

I'm too confused to be hurt by her words. "As should you." I give her a wink as I stand, but she turns her head before she can see it. Maybe this is part of her plan or maybe she is really upset for some reason. Whatever it is, I can't resist a final playful jab as I walk out of the door. "Tell Peter I said hello."

☦ CHAPTER SEVEN ☦

Mother Wolfe sits at the desk near the front door. When I approach, she quickly slips the book she was reading into her bag. I'd like to know what was in the book that caused her cheeks to flush crimson, but she doesn't seem like she wants to share it with me.

"Are you going out?" Her voice is a notch higher than normal.

"Is that alright?" I smile sweetly.

"Of course," she gushes. "Did you want an escort? It's easy to get lost around here."

Rosemary opens the door and the wind follows her inside the dome. The two women exchange a silent look before Mother Wolfe returns her attention to me. "I see. Well, have a good time. If you need anything just ask one of the citizens to call the Welcome Center and I'll send someone to help."

"She'll be fine." Rosemary rolls her eyes as she tugs on my arm. "She isn't like the others."

Mother Wolfe sighs dramatically as if she is really my mother. "I know that, but I still worry."

I'm tempted to roll my eyes too. "Thank you, Mother Wolfe. I promise to get in touch if I need something. I shouldn't be out too late."

"You're a good girl." She nods and tears fill her eyes. "I can't believe you had to survive outside the wall for that long."

*

"What do you mean when you say that I'm not like the others?" The light is fading, illuminating everything in a golden tint and giving Rosemary a sun kissed glow on her too pale skin.

She turns to look away from me as we cross the main road. "I'm sorry, I'm not trying to insult anyone. It's just that you adapt so easily and you're not…" Her voice trails off as she struggles to find the words. "You're not old and weird."

"Weird?" *That's the word she chooses?*

"Ugh," she groans as she scuffs her shoes against the sidewalk. "Different, maybe? The other ones who come are smart, don't get me wrong, but they don't seem to fit in. It's like you already belong here. The way you move and talk is a little different than the rest of us, but it isn't that noticeable. You carry yourself in the way we were all taught to act. Honestly, you'd probably make a good Sister or Mother."

Her smile is a proud one. She thinks she's given me a great compliment. I lower my eyes so I don't glare at her. Maybe it isn't her fault. Maybe they were all taught to be this ignorant.

"Plus," she continues as she wraps her arm around my shoulders. "You did save the life of a watchman. That makes you sort of a hero. The other girls are really excited to meet you."

*

This dome sits far removed from the main street, tucked behind a row of trees with a rocky path leading to the doorway. As we head down the path, notes of music drift through the evening air to greet us. The music reminds me of Calder's guitar, but magnified, like there are multiple guitars being played by many musicians to make one song. I can't help but walk faster as an honest grin brightens my face.

"Do you like music?" Rosemary laughs as she hurries to catch up.

"I do." And in this moment, I think I genuinely like her too for bringing me somewhere where the music plays.

*

It's a tavern, well, sort of a tavern. The smell of alcohol permeates the building, mixing with the coppery burning meat scent that rides on the smoke drifting through the air. My eyelids flutter, adjusting to the dim lights, as the music wraps around my body. It pulls me deeper inside the dome and sets every nerve I have on fire.

A few men gather around the bar counter, but the rest of the room is filled with young women lounging on soft chairs or spread out on colorful pillows that line the walls and sipping from glass cups so delicate that they reflect the golden lightbulbs hanging from the ceiling. Some puff on long tubes, sending trails of smoke dancing around me as it tries to escape through the open door.

It's a tavern, yet it's not a tavern. Music fills the room instead of laughter. The men don't jostle one another and the women sit with cold, calculating eyes as they watch me pass. I pull at the edge of my sleeves and try to ignore their curious looks. Even in this half-light, I can see they all wear white.

"There you are!" a woman exclaims as she reaches for Rosemary. Her hair is loose, dark ringlets fall like a curtain around her shoulders, and her eyes are glazed to match the wobble in her stance. "It took you forever to get here so we ordered your food already. It was worth it though." She glances over Rosemary's shoulder, giving me a look more intense than I'd imagined she could give in this altered state. "We are all just dying to meet the famous Brooke."

"Did you drink before eating, Maisy?" Rosemary laughs nervously as she casts a sympathetic smile my way. "We don't need to overwhelm Brooke before she even has a chance to sit down."

"No, that's alright." I shake my head. "Maisy, is it? Nice to meet you. Except I don't know what is so exciting about you meeting me."

"Are you kidding?" Maisy cries out as she pulls me past Rosemary and onto the circular booth seat lined with a red plush cushion. "Everyone has heard about you. The girl who dragged Calder for miles through the middle of the night and saved his life. I half expected you to be ten foot tall with the biceps of a man, but you are such a pretty little thing. It's all so glamourous."

Her compliment makes me uncomfortable. I shift my eyes around the table to see five other women cradling their drinks and hanging on Maisy's every word. Well, all of them except Sister Auburn. I didn't realize she would be here. She gives me a guilty smile.

"Then Charlotte here told us how smart you are," Maisy continues to gush. "You're already a legend. No wonder Calder brought you back."

The heat rushes to my face. I don't want any of this attention. Rosemary hangs her head in defeat as she slides into the booth next to me.

"Sorry," she whispers. "I didn't mean to put you through this right away."

"Nonsense." Maisy slaps her palm against the worn wood table and then instantly pulls it into the air, shaking it to relieve the pain.

"Ouch, that kind of hurt," she giggles. "What I meant to say is don't be ridiculous. Brooke has nothing to worry about. We are all grateful for her, especially for saving our Calder."

Our Calder. There's a sharp edge behind her playful words that I don't understand. A history not written in the library books. I suck in a breath between my teeth, trying not to let the discomfort show on my face.

"Really, you've got me all wrong." I shrug with one shoulder and glance up at the delicate lights hanging around the room. "I only did what any caring person would do. I couldn't leave him out there to die."

This is news to Maisy. She rests her elbow on the table and lays her chin in the curve of her hand. "So, he didn't choose you?"

The question is full of accusation and I'll be damned if I know what I did to deserve it. The other women's eyes widen, waiting for my response. Rosemary bites her lip to hide the secret smile that accompanies the story she's made up in her head. Only Charlotte, Sister Auburn, seems out of place here as her eyes dart around to everywhere but this table.

"Oh gods no," I laugh dismissively. "He's the most annoying creature I've ever met and I'm pretty sure he feels the same way about me."

The other girls at the table relax. This is all they needed to know. Their eyes glaze over as they sip their drinks, listening to the delicious music that overrides our voices. It's almost dreamlike how easily they can adjust from one reality to the next.

But Maisy lingers, still unsure of how to process my response. "Why him?" she asks. "And why you?"

"I'm not sure." I turn to stare her straight in the eyes and the effect is so much more satisfying than I'd imagined. She seems to sweat under my gaze. "He didn't want to bring me here and I didn't know I was coming. They said because I can read and paint that I didn't belong outside the wall."

"They were right." Maisy nods, lifting her glass in salute. "I think you belong right here with us." I look to her drink and to my own empty hand.

"Maybe," I laugh as sweetly as I can, trying not to let my sarcasm leak through. "But I'll need a drink first. If you'll excuse me, I'll go get one now."

There's a commotion behind me as I stand from the table, but the anger that causes my teeth to clench doesn't permit me to care. Charlotte's voice rises above the music, assuring Rosemary that she's "got this" and forcing her to sit back down. I keep my head held high as I walk alone to the bar.

"Don't worry about Maisy," Charlotte whispers as she places an arm over my shoulder.

"She's always had a thing for my brother. A lot of the girls did."

I resist the urge to shrug her off and nod instead. "I figured something like that was happening."

"I didn't know you were coming until I got here or else I would have warned you," Charlotte sighs. "It's not really that big of a deal. Calder never liked her. The girls just make silly claims on men when they leave for the watch. It doesn't always work out like they hope though."

"Aren't they just boys when they leave for the watch?" I can't help but ask the question. The men at the bar scoot away when we get there, giving us plenty of space to order at the counter.

"Not really boys," Charlotte explains. "They are already getting into trouble at that age." I think of Tordon and I sneaking around, taking Aegir's boats out for joyrides when we were sixteen. *Gods, was that really three years ago.*

"And the women don't get into trouble?" I hide my smirk by glancing over my shoulder to where Maisy sits at the table engrossed in conversation with the other girls. Her hands move wildly in the air as she crafts a story. Then my eyes travel around the room before returning back to Charlotte. It hits me that the only men in the building are sitting right here at the bar.

"Girls don't get in trouble the way boys do." Charlotte motions to the bartender. His brown beard is trimmed neatly, accenting the sharp curve of his jaw.

"What will it be, sisters?" he asks.

"I'm not a Sister." The response falls from my open mouth which I quickly snap closed, hoping no one heard the disdain in my voice. I'm going to have to get better at playing along if I want to fit in here. Maisy set me on edge. I can't let that happen again.

"It's just a friendly greeting," Charlotte laughs. "All women are either called mothers or sisters. It's only when you take a position on the council that the official title gets tied to your name."

"Do all of them work on the council?" I glance back to the table. Maisy is still talking.

"No." Charlotte shakes her head. "Just me. And to be honest, I think they are starting to hate me for it. We've all been friends our whole lives and graduated together, but maybe sometimes people grow apart."

I ponder this new information as I study the row of bottles illuminated behind the bartender. The light gives him a hazy glow. His beard is nice and I appreciate looking at it. It's weird how facial hair seems so out place here when it was all I knew at home.

"Do you have any rum?" I ask quickly, embarrassed to find myself staring at him.

"I'm not sure what that is," he answers slowly as he looks to the bottles on the shelf.

"Let's get you some wine," Charlotte giggles. "We can bring a few bottles to the table. My treat."

The bartender hurries to get us glasses and find whatever it was she ordered. The music rolls across my skin as we wait.

"There are no musicians here, are there?" I ask after another song begins to play.

"No, it's all electronic," she explains. "But if you like music I can take you to a show sometime."

"That would be nice." I return her smile. "Also, why are there no men sitting in the comfortable chairs?" The men at the bar stare down into their drinks. I wonder if they've heard my question.

"This place is mostly a singles club." She takes the glasses and bottles filled with a deep red liquid from the counter. "Men have a two-drink maximum when they are alone in bars. If they were here with their wives, they'd be allowed to sit wherever they wanted."

"Seriously?" My jaw drops to the floor. "Why is that?"

"Their biology doesn't mix well with alcohol. It's for the safety of everyone to regulate how much they consume," Charlotte states this like a common truth. I have to stop myself from laughing.

I turn to look at the bar again. The man who moved when I came to order at the counter gives me a knowing look, staring deep into my eyes as if he wants to speak, and then downs his drink in a single gulp before standing up and walking away.

*

The wine is sweet. It coats my tongue and the back of my throat before sending warmth to my stomach. It's not as strong as rum, but the effect is enough to loosen the tension from my shoulders and amplify the vibration from the music that is not really being played here. The dim lights remind me of lantern glow and I'm grateful they aren't so blinding.

This moment would almost be peaceful, if the girls at the table weren't eager to ask me every question they can think of.

"What is it like living out there?" Paige, or maybe it's Sage, asks. Her hair is tied into two separate braids and the alcohol makes her nose pink. She seems too young to be here.

"It's hard," I answer because that's what they want to hear. "We are always working. In the cold season when the fish aren't as plentiful near the coast and the sea birds aren't laying eggs we have to travel further out on the ocean. This is when they hunt for whales. Those trips are even harder. Boats work together to wrangle the beasts, and not everyone makes it back, but the oil and fat sustains us through the year."

"Whales?" Paige/Sage gasps. "Did you know they were once endangered?"

"Not anymore." I smile as I take another sip of my wine. "Now they outnumber us ten to one and wouldn't hesitate to capsize one of our boats just for fun."

"How did you learn to read?" Maisy asks. She's been clinging to my side since I sat down. "I thought no one outside the wall knew how."

The question feels like a trap. I roll the liquid, squeezed from grapes grown in the outermost fields of the district, around in my mouth to stall while I think of the right words to say.

"Nobody does," I finally answer. "At least, I don't think that they do. I just picked it up from old labeled parts and trash that our divers recover from the bottom of the sea." It isn't fully a lie, just mostly.

This sets off a myriad of questions and I laugh as I try to answer each one. Charlotte is silent as she watches me talk. Her gaze makes me nervous. Her eyes are so much like Calder's. I stick to the truth as closely as I can so as not to arouse suspicion. They can't know about Meghan. I have to protect my sister at all costs. If they knew my father taught me to read, they could easily assume he taught her too.

"I have a question," I say playfully as I reach for the bottle to refill my glass. "Why do you think more people on the wall haven't learned how to read? I mean, I'm no one special."

This question causes them to frown and avert their eyes. I mentally kick myself for asking it and set down the glass. No one seems to know the answer, even Charlotte in all her knowledge pretends to study the nails on her fingers.

Maisy pours the rest of the bottle into her glass and signals the waiter for another. "Learning to read takes education." Maisy glances to Charlotte and shakes her head before continuing, "Normally you are taught for years to read. Except you. You, my dear, are some kind of genius." She pauses to wink at me. "It's better that they don't know how to read, right? What kind of life would that be? Knowing how to read but having nothing to read."

The other girls nod in agreement. The sweetness of the wine turns sour on my tongue. There is something they aren't telling me, but I'll never know what it is if I remain an outsider.

"You are so right." I raise my glass in salute to her empty one. "It was awful knowing how to read and having nothing to practice with."

Maisy beams with a perfectly white and even toothed smile that shines through the dimly lit room. "I told you that you belonged here."

The girls want more information and who can blame them? From the questions they ask and the wonder in their eyes, it seems they've lived very sheltered lives inside the wall. The more they want to know, the more exotic I seem to them. Maisy doesn't like this. She shifts uncomfortably in her seat and orders yet another drink. I get a small bit of self-satisfaction from sensing her squirm. Of course, I wouldn't say anything directly, but it amuses me nonetheless.

"Honestly." Rosemary lays a gentle hand on my arm. She's had a few drinks since we arrived and tears are forming in her eyes. "It all seems so barbaric to me. I'm hurt that you had to live there. You didn't deserve that kind of life."

No one deserves that kind of life, I want to scream. But maybe this is my fault. In my haste to give them what they wanted I did a disservice to my people. There is more to life than just surviving. It's not as cutthroat as my dry words led them to believe.

"It wasn't all bad," I whisper as the girls strain their ears to hear me speak. "Sometimes when the fog rolls in like a heavy blanket, the horns from the boats call to one another guiding each other home like a haunting melody of protection. And when the sun sets every night, it lights up the horizon and the water with the most beautiful hue of orangish reds that can't be replicated by paint. After a raging storm, the people open their shutters and celebrate the entire day because we are alive. And the spinners, where I used to work, sit on the rocks all day weaving ropes and singing in voices so ethereal that the sound drifts to the fat white clouds and reaches the gods in the heavens. We carry each other when one of us is broken. We fight hard and we love hard, because we know that life isn't guaranteed."

"What about the men?" Maisy smirks, breaking the trancelike concentration of the girls.

"What about them?" I sigh. The wine is making me tired of all this.

"Are they cute?" she asks. The girls perk up, scooting to the edge of their seats. It dawns on me that they don't ever see men their own age, and the ones they do see are just playthings to them. *Gods, forgive me for what I'm about to do.*

"Oh yes, they are beyond handsome." I smile mischievously. "Rough calloused hands with big hearts. Like Tordon, my best friend, the muscles ripple beneath his bronze skin and his clear blue eyes rival the color of the sky. When he stands on the edge of the boat, his silhouette backdropped by the raging sea, and he pulls in the heavy soaked nets while turning to give you a playful grin- he could very well be a god on earth. He is tough, but he has a fiercely protective love for his family."

The memory of Endre's lifeless body being pulled from the wreckage of the *Hronn* threatens to crush my heart all over again, but I smile through the pain and hurry to add, "All the men are like this."

The girls are practically salivating, licking their lips and nervously sipping their wine. Part of me feels guilty for turning Tordon into their fantasy, but I don't think he'd mind that much. Maybe Lena might. But even Maisy has melted. She runs her finger around the rim of the glass, lost in thought and staring off into the distance.

"Do you miss it?" Rosemary whispers.

I'm not sure that anyone has heard her question, but I choose my answer carefully. "My place is here now."

*

The girls all had too much to drink. It's comical to watch them stumble over each other as they cling to outstretched arms. I can't help but glance over my shoulder, waiting for a watchman to step in and ask if there is a problem. But I'm being ridiculous. I know where the watchmen are, where all the men are, and that is not here.

The moon is high in the sky by the time we tumble as a group out the door of the dome. My breath comes out in puffs of smoke and I inhale the crisp air, letting it fill my lungs and clear my mind. Maisy hiccups as she leans against a fence post. Her perfect ringlets are frizzed and wild around her reddened cheeks.

"You know," she laughs drunkenly, clinging to the post for support. "It's a good thing Calder didn't get you pregnant and bring you here. Could you imagine how High Mother Auburn would have handled that?"

This question sets off a fit of giggles. Charlotte looks away embarrassed as Rosemary trips and grabs for my arm. I'm forced to hold her upright so we both don't fall.

"Is she really that bad?" I smile as I ask. Their laughter is contagious.

Maisy blows me a kiss as she stumbles away down the path opposite of the one we are taking. "Just be glad you'll never have to find out."

✟ CHAPTER EIGHT ✟

My throat is so dry I could swallow the entire ocean. I have a brief moment of panic where I wonder if I've been poisoned, but the sickening taste of wine still coats my teeth. *That was a poison in itself.*

"Are you planning to get up today?" Jillian's voice calls to me from the foot of the bed. I peer out over the top of the blanket, letting my eyes adjust to the daylight in the room.

"Did I miss breakfast?" Even my words are dry.

"You did." Jillian folds her arms over her chest. "But I'm sure the staff will whip something special up just for you." The insult hangs in the air.

"Did I do something wrong?" I sit up slowly.

"No." Jillian sighs as anger deflates from her sails. "You're doing exactly what you are supposed to do. Maybe next time you shouldn't drink so much though."

"The wine is poison," I groan as I put my feet onto the floor. "It just snuck up on me."

"Next time ask for beer," Jillian chuckles. "It's nowhere near as good as Aegir makes, but it's better than the grape syrup."

*

They are cleaning up the cafeteria when I poke my head in through the open door. Mercury catches sight of me and waves me over.

"See. Told you," Jillian mutters as she waits in the hall.

"I was going to have this brought to your room." Mercury gives me a knowing smile as he hands me a hunk of sausage wrapped in bread and a glass of orange juice. I gratefully swallow the liquid in a single gulp. Apparently chugging water from the bathroom faucet for five minutes wasn't enough to quench my thirst.

"Thank you." I place the empty glass in the wash basin and cradle the food to my chest. "I could kiss you right now."

Mercury smiles a devilish grin, his whiskered lip curving as he gives me a wink, and then laughs as he returns to washing dishes.

*

"Where are you two off to this morning?" Mother Wolfe catches us at the door. Her disapproving look toward Jillian quickly changes to concern when she turns to me.

"I'm going to show Brooke the greenhouse if that's okay." Jillian's voice is suddenly sweet, almost as deceptive as the taste of wine. It even takes Mother Wolfe by surprise.

"Of course," she exclaims, rushing to the door to open it for us. Jillian breezes straight through, but Mother Wolfe gently holds me back by my arm.

"Are you alright?" she asks. "You don't look like yourself today."

I grin sheepishly, the embarrassment causing my shoulders to sag. "I just had a little too much wine with my fun last night. It won't happen again."

"Oh, Brooke," she laughs heartily as she rubs my arm. "You have as much fun and as much wine as you like. What I wouldn't give to be young and free again. No marriage, no responsibilities- enjoy it while it lasts. Soon you'll be settled down and boring just like I am."

I leave her standing there smiling and waving as I hurry to catch up with Jillian. Confusion clouds my already foggy brain. Somehow, I've made Mother Wolfe like me more and all I did was drink too much.

*

Heavy doors seal behind us in the clear dome made of see-through plastic. It's warm and sticky in here, like being on the ocean in the middle of summer on a rare day without a breeze. Green plants climb each other, growing on posts taller than my head. The distinct sound of rushing water runs along the tubing on the floor. We are in a lush forest of edible produce.

"Did you do all this?" I gasp, remembering her house with rows of PVC piping connected to her market stall. We all thought she was magic- her and her mother both- for growing plants with no soil, but this level of growth is unbelievable.

"No." Jillian shakes her head as she leads us deeper into the maze of greenery. "My mother started it. They were using a hydroponic system for years but apparently it was causing too much damage to the environment with the fertilizers it involved. They took my ma because she understood aquaponics and they didn't."

"Is Vera here?" I turn to look around the greenhouse, but I can't see anything through the rows of plants.

Jillian approaches a work bench littered with gardening tools and leans against it. "Would you mind getting that bucket for me? My back hurts today." She points to a yellow plastic container with a handle on it just a few inches away from her hand. I eye her skeptically as I lean down to retrieve it.

Just as I bend over, she reaches her hand underneath the table and begins to tap against it frantically. I look up to see a message etched into the wood:

I did everything I could to get you here.

My eyes feel like they are going to pop out of my head as I stand back up. "What did she do?"

Jillian places a finger over her lips and takes the bucket from my hand.

In the back of the greenhouse are tanks of water filled with fish darting close to the looking glass and disappearing back into the murky depths. I smile as I watch them play.

Jillian shakes her head and sighs. "My mother tried to explain to these idiots that salmon need warm water."

"That's not right," I interject. "Salmon are…"

She cuts me off with a raised eyebrow and conspiratorial smile. "They know nothing of fish here on the land," she continues. "They couldn't keep the salmon alive after she passed away. They tossed in some fresh water fish called trout but didn't bother to regulate the salinity of the tanks first. Those didn't last long either. Now I've got them using blue tilapia. They're almost as easy to maintain as the tilapia back home."

"I'm sorry about your mother." I leave the fish to stand by her side. The water gurgles around us, filling the room with life.

"Don't be." She shrugs. "I said my goodbyes years ago when I thought she chose to retire. In a way she's the only one who got to live out that dream and now I get to have it too. I only wish we'd known the truth so that I could warn my half-wit brother, but you can't change the past."

"We can try to change the future though." I bump my shoulder against hers, hoping to cheer her up.

She stares at the tanks for a moment before nodding, then picks up the bucket and begins to feed the fish.

*

Peter asked Jillian to meet him for lunch, she'd guiltily explained to me. I don't know why she feels the need to apologize. If we are going to be stuck living here for the foreseeable future, then we might as well enjoy ourselves a little bit.

But is this a betrayal to my family? The thought nags me as I walk alone down the dirt path through the empty fields. Meghan must be so worried right now. I hope Lena and Tordon are checking on her. My eyes fill with tears when I think of Zander asking why I don't come around anymore. I inhale deeply to stop this train of thought. If I let myself live in the pain of missing them then I know I'll die in it.

This is what I was doing by questioning my father's death, living in the pain and hoping beyond all hope that he was still alive somewhere. But I know

now it doesn't matter, the pain of being separated from those you love feels the same.

No, it's not. I ignore these depressing thoughts. *I will see Meghan again someday.* I blink my eyes until they are dry and lower my face to focus on the path I walk on now. The dirt crunches and crumbles under my shoes. I still can't believe how much dirt exists here. I kick a small rock, sending it flying into the drying grass.

Footsteps approach loudly from behind, snapping me from my internal reflection. I turn to find a man ambling down the path as quickly as he can while leaning on a cane. My first thought is to quicken my pace, I can easily outrun him, but he holds up his hand and calls out my name.

It's Charles, the first person I met when I came to this strange world. Yet his face looks different. It takes me a moment to register that he now wears glasses.

"Nice day for a walk, isn't it?" he asks as he catches up to me. His voice is so direct and his eyes are so large under the magnifying lenses. It's a change from his normal shifty demeanor, standing dutifully behind his wife and casting nervous glances my way.

Instinctively, I take a step back. Something is not right with him. He notices my hesitation.

"My apologies." He bows his head. "I wasn't trying to frighten you. I just had to make sure."

"Make sure of what?" I glance around the open field. Somehow, I drifted far away from the domes and city center while I was lost in thought. There's no one out here but the two of us.

"My eyes are bad," he hurries to explain. "When I first saw you, I was sure they were playing tricks on me. Mother Neil finally convinced me to get glasses. I've been stubborn about it, but now I have a good reason."

"What reason is that?" I continue inching backwards. If I need to take off running, I want to be out of reach of his arm and his cane.

"I had to see you." He steps forward urgently and I take another step back. "I had to prove to myself you weren't a ghost. But you are real and you look just like her. Do you remember the name of the gate near your city?"

Curiosity fixes me to the spot. I bite my lip as I study his face, trying to decide if he is dangerous or just delusional. *What harm can it do to tell him where I'm from?* It's not like he can get there now. I remember the words labeled on Calder's map still safely tucked inside my dress. "The Island Gate."

"I knew it!" Charles suddenly pumps his fist in the air causing me to jump. "No, no. Don't be frightened." He lowers his voice. "Do you know a woman name Ligeia? She has to be related to you."

Now he has my full attention. "Ligeia was my grandmother."

A smile spreads across his face, pinching the wrinkles by his eyes together. "So the baby, Leif was his name I think, is he your father?"

"Was my father." I eye the old man warily, unsure of where this is going. "He died earlier this year."

"Oh no." Charles looks heartbroken. "That's a shame. Is Ligeia still alive?"

"No." I shake my head, remembering her burial at sea and my father refusing to let us cry. "She died when I was a small child."

Tears form in his eyes and he removes his glasses to wipe them away. "I'm sorry to hear this. You've dealt with a great amount of loss for being so young."

I raise my chin, refusing to accept his pity. "How do you know my grandmother?"

"You even stand like her." He smiles sadly. "I didn't know her all that well. Truthfully, none of us did. But there is a man I know who would have done anything for her. Tell me, did she ever remarry?"

"No, she didn't." I fold my arms over my chest. "What man are you talking about?" *He better not be insinuating anything about my grandmother.*

"I promise to take you to him one day." A loud beeping emits from his pocket, interrupting the explanation. He pulls out a box- *a short range radio that works on... magic-* and presses the device to his ear.

"Yes, mother dearest," he says. "I've just now caught up to her and am sending her that way."

He drops the device in his pocket and shakes his head as if emerging from a dream. "Mother Neil sent me to tell you that Calder is awake and asking for you at the hospital."

The mention of Calder's name sends a rush of warmth to my stomach that makes me blush. Charles pretends not to notice, but he can't hide his widening eyes behind his new glasses.

"Why don't you run ahead?" He sighs, tapping his cane against the ground. "My legs aren't what they used to be either."

"What man are you talking about?" I force myself to stand perfectly still despite every nerve in my body telling me to run. I try to reason that I just want to be done with this conversation, but even the damn wind is pulling me towards the hospital.

"I promise to tell you more later. We don't have enough time to talk today. Just know I made a mistake a long time ago and I want the chance to fix things. You should go to the hospital." He turns to hobble down the path, taking one last look over his shoulder. "And Brooke, just for now, let's keep this between the two of us."

What is wrong with me? I should chase after that crazy old man, demand that he explains how he knows my grandmother, and make him tell me what he did to her.

But I don't.

My lungs burn as I race to the hospital. *Is Calder really awake this time? Will he say the same things twice?* Not that I care, of course. It's just that being near him feels like a connection to my life outside of this wall. And I want to make sure he is okay.

I chase a faint daydream as I run through the open field back to the city. I can take him to get an almond croissant- *Charlotte said it's his favorite*- and maybe I'll be able to connect with him, reassure him that the way he is being treated is not okay. Boys don't deserve to be sent away just because of their *biology*. I'd leave my family a thousand times if it meant stopping him, or any other child, from being ripped away from their home. The very thought of this sickens me. And I see Calder in my mind, with all his strength, his stoic face, his goofy smile, the music he plays- it all swirls into a colorful picture that I want to keep. *He doesn't deserve this kind of life.*

I pause, dropping my hands to my knees, panting heavily and trying to get in enough air to compose myself. *It's just the idea of him that excites me.* I want to go home and he is my tether to the real world. When he gets better then he might be able to help.

No. I shake my head to dispel the fantasy. He said he wanted to understand things, but he is no one in this world of women. *Well then, maybe I need to protect him.*

It's painful how slow I force myself to walk now that the gleaming white dome of the hospital is in sight. They don't need to see me rushing. I don't want any more rumors spread. Calder is just a watchman. I have no real connection to him.

And yet… The slightest nagging whisper of the word *yet.* A smile curls my lips anyway. I can't wait to tease him about wanting to hold my hand.

*

"He doesn't want to see you." Mother Morgana Auburn, High Council Leader of the District of the Americas, stands outside Calder's door. She seems much taller than I remember, or maybe I've grown smaller. Whatever the case, she folds her arms over her tall, thin body and stares down at me past her straight nose. Her eyes, *Calder's eyes,* gleam with a protectiveness that makes me feel disgusting in my own skin.

"I was told to come here," I whisper anxiously. Calder is just behind her in the room. If I could force myself to speak louder, he might hear me. He'd know I was here. But I'm afraid to cause a commotion. Jillian's words are drilled into my head. *I need to earn my whites to be heard.* And looking at Mother Auburn now, it appears I'll need to earn much more than that.

Mother Auburn sighs as she rubs a hand across the back of her neck. Her fingernails are perfectly shaped into crescent moons, clean and clear of work, but her reddish hair tinted with gray is coming loose from her strict bun. She looks like her children and at the same time, she doesn't look like them at all.

"Listen to me, child. I'm grateful that you saved his life. I wouldn't have expected a savage to do that, but in this one instance I'm happy to have been proven wrong." I clench my teeth at the insult, but she doesn't notice or pretends not to.

"It was wrong of me not to thank you when you arrived," Mother Auburn continues. "But seeing a child of yours in such a vulnerable state brings out something irrational. Almost barbaric, which I'm sure you understand."

I suck in a deep breath and force myself to remain silent. She isn't done insulting me yet, I'd be a fool to think otherwise.

"And the implications of you two coming back in the middle of the night, it's enough to make a mother's heart stop." She waves her hand dismissively, blowing away the worry with a slight shift of her slender fingers in the air.

"Never mind that now. I spoke with Henry and know the circumstances surrounding your arrival. It seems you already made an impression with the citizens and I won't deprive them of their entertainment. But hear me now." She lowers her voice as she looks me in the eyes. "If you want to earn your whites, and I'm told you are on the fast track to getting them, then you will promise to stay away from my son."

I nod, not trusting myself to speak, as I turn on my heel to leave. *Did he hear her talking to me?* I feel so deflated. Every part of me wants to push her to the side and do what I came here to do. I want to see Calder. Whatever I did to earn that woman's scorn doesn't justify not letting me visit him. *I dragged him for five miles and saved his life, for gods' sakes.*

Anger fumes from my shoulders as I force myself to walk softly, slowly exiting the building as if nothing is wrong. *Screw Calder and his possessive mother.* He must have heard her speaking and he said nothing. I knew better than to trust a watchman. It was stupid of me to get sidetracked. The end goal here is to earn these ridiculous whites and be given a voice again. Nothing is going to stop me from that.

✟ CHAPTER NINE ✟

Mother Wolfe smiles brightly as I enter the Welcome Center. I resist the urge to glare at her and settle for a courteous nod instead.

She can't seem to control herself any longer and the words come rushing from her painted lips, "You have a gift waiting for you in your room. I hope you don't mind the intrusion to your personal space, but the instructions were to assemble it for you."

"A gift?" My eyebrows raise. "From who?"

"It didn't say." She jumps up from the cushioned seat and starts walking down the hall, beckoning me forward with a curled finger.

I sigh deeply as I follow her. Apparently, she can't resist the urge to take part in whatever spectacle this is. I don't expect her to let me open my own door, but at the last minute she steps aside and lowers her eyes guiltily. Her enthusiasm makes her seem so innocent. I have to remind myself it isn't her fault that Mother Auburn is such a bitch.

When I open the door to my room, a cry of joy makes me clasp my hands over my lips. A wooden stand holds a blank canvas. Paint and brushes are arranged on the small table by its side, more colorful and vibrant than a bouquet of flowers. There's a thick stack of more blank canvases waiting to be filled in sitting on the floor against the wall.

"Who did this?" I can't believe there are tears in my eyes. It takes everything in me not to rush across the room and hug the brushes to my chest.

"I set it up," Mother Wolfe explains proudly. "But I don't know who sent it. There's a sealed note placed between the paint jars. I didn't dare open it though. That's naturally none of my business."

"Thank you." I turn to smile at her. She lingers by the door, the disappointment that I'm not opening the note in her presence is written clearly on her face.

"Well, I'll leave you to it." She nods after an awkward moment of silence. "We are all so excited to see what you will create."

The note feels heavy in my hand, not the weight of it but the implication. I should open it, except I'm nervous. *Would that weird old man have gotten me paints?* The thought of it worries me. I don't want to let Charles be a part of my life. He seems untrustworthy and I worry about what he meant in the field today. I wonder if he hurt my grandmother. But maybe he is being cryptic. Ligeia was always so strong and she never spoke bad about the watchmen to me. If Charles really did know my grandmother, then it would be nice to speak with him again. Though there is something about his shifting eyes and secrets behind his words that make me uncomfortable. *If he was the one who sent the paints, I'm going to have to send them back.*

I console myself with the fact that it's probably from Rosemary or Charlotte. Either of them would be kind enough to do this for me. They are both so sweet and I don't want to like them, but I'd be lying if I didn't. It's probably from Charlotte. Her attempt at making up for Maisy and also encouraging me to start painting again.

The note falls open from my hand as it drifts down to the floor. I clench my teeth as I stare out through the open window. There's no name on the page, but I would recognize that handwriting anywhere.

For the nightmares, it says.

Curse that stupid, thick skulled watchman.

I should send this all to the hospital just to spite him. How dare he let his mother speak to me in that way and then send gifts to me in secret? To be fair, he probably sent this before her one-sided conversation. *But still!* He doesn't care about my nightmares; he doesn't care at all. He basically abandoned me in this strange world while he lies, unreachable now, in a hospital bed.

I need to get away from the paint before I'm tempted to use it. The door slams a little too hard behind me and I grip the handle, checking the empty hall to make sure no one heard it.

The watchman can't get under my skin. I refuse to give him that kind of power anymore. *Deep breaths and gentle footsteps.* I have a job to do.

The cafeteria is filled with a different kind of energy tonight. Eyes shift toward me and nervous smiles are given everywhere I look. *They're all watching me.* My heart beats rapidly in my chest, but I force my hands to stay steady as I tightly grip the tray. Mercury gives me a large helping of the pasta dish and tops it off with a playful wink. Confused, I carry the tray to where Jillian sits and try my hardest to ignore their eyes as I pass.

"What's going on?" I whisper as I take the seat next to hers.

"It seems like the resident artist got some paints. Now everyone is waiting to see what you can do," Jillian smirks as my jaw drops.

"What do they expect from me?" I glance around the cafeteria. The citizens-in-training return their attention to their food when I catch them staring. Mother Wolfe stands at the open door with another woman. They speak in hushed tones as they watch me. When she sees me looking, she gives me a short wave and a proud smile spreads across her face.

"I don't know." Jillian shrugs. "But whatever it is better be worthy of all this attention."

I've never hated Calder more in my life then I do right this moment.

*

Alone in my room, I trail my fingers over the tops of the glass jars. Calder did well with choosing these colors. The larger containers hold tints of blue, red, and yellow. I wonder if he knew I can make any color with these. *Probably not, it took years for me to figure that out.* I have everything I could ever need here. Except everyone I love.

The pain passes through me as I breathe deeply. I pick up one of the brushes to inspect. These are nothing like the ones I have back at home. I'm not even sure that the bristles are hair because they are so tightly bound to the wood pole. The entire thing feels lightweight in my hand, like I could paint clouds with a delicate stroke.

I toss the brush back into the jar and hug my arms against my body while I walk over to the bed. The mattress catches me as I sit contemplating this whole situation. *Why did Calder do this to me?* I don't even know what they want me to paint.

Everything I've done so far has been pieces of my life, paintings of the sea, and I don't think that's what they want. These people are so caught up in their perfect world. My world would destroy them. A nagging voice tells me to forget this all, they can't force me to do anything. They can't have this part of me if I don't want to give it. *Curse them all and curse that watchman. I'm never going to paint again.*

*

The wharf is empty. It takes a moment for this to register as the surreal landscape swirls around me. The wharf is never empty, but it is now- I can prove it. Something bad must have happened. Something I don't know about.

Of course I don't know, I chide myself. *I'm so far away now that I'd never hear the sirens.*

I walk down the pier, dreamlike and slow, as the full moon illuminates the rusted metal planks beneath my feet. If there is no one here, why does it feel like a thousand eyes are watching my every move? I grip the rail tightly, feeling the cool metal against my palm.

If I turn around then I know I'll see them. The eyes of the watchmen peering at me from the shadows. Even Calder is there. I can feel his gaze like a knife in my back.

The dark water reflecting the moonlight on the surface laps at the poles that uphold the pier. Each wave washes against the crustaceans and algae that have attached themselves to the support beams. If I jump into the water, I can escape this torture. The watching eyes will disappear.

But in this moment, I feel Zander's body in my arms, clinging to me like he did on the day I slipped from the wharf. *"Breathe baby, breathe,"* a voice calls out from over the water that no longer sounds like my own.

*

I gasp, sitting upright in the bed, as the soft blankets fall in puddles around me. The moon is so full that it forces itself through the slats of the blinds and illuminates the canvas across the room. I pull my knees to my chest, anxious to dispel the lingering fears from the dream. The canvas calls to me, but I don't leave the warmth of the bed.

They want something I don't want to give. They want me to make a show of myself. Whatever I paint will be judged and I have no doubt this will be a part of earning my whites. Why Calder gave this to me is a mystery, but I can't let the opportunity slip through my fingers. I rub my palms hard against my sleep crusted eyes.

Think. I need to think. I'm not cocky enough to think I can win them over with my simple paintings when I've seen their art in the museum. I'll have to do something that connects with them, something that will make them love it.

But how? I struggle to think through the fog of sleep. What can I paint to impress them? I think of their eyes, of the watchmen's eyes, and they all blur together into a nightmarish monster. A monster that sits staring and waiting to see something. What is it looking for?

Nothing, I chuckle to myself as I pull the blanket higher on my shoulders and wrap it around my body. They want to see nothing. They want comfort and compliancy. They want everything to be what they feel is right. And just like they expect me to accept their world without question, they need to validate their existence. The pristinely white clothes and the perfect smiles- it all makes sense to me now. They feel they are superior, flawless, and I need to give them proof that they are. I already gave it once by saving the watchman and I'm doing it now by behaving in the way they hoped.

I clench my jaw as I accept this truth. I can't think of another way around it. By the light of the moon dancing on the canvas, the image becomes clear to me now. I know what I need to paint to earn my whites.

*

The canvas gleams in the morning sun that brightens the bedroom. I had to turn off the electric lights. The paint didn't look right under their glow. The material of the canvas itself is different, porous in a way, and it'll be harder to push the paint around then it is on the fiberglass sheets I'm accustomed to using. This worries me a bit. I won't be able to make many mistakes.

I envision the complete painting inside my head. It helps that I've already seen what to paint. It won't be exactly what I imagined, that's not what they would want to see, but it'll still be mine. That gives me enough motivation to start.

"Is she pretty?" The warm memory flows through my blood and releases itself through the paintbrush extending from my hand. *Emotions.* As deep as the sea and as old as the earth. So big they can fill a small, broken shack with laughter. Expressing themselves through your eyes.

Eyes are not just for watching. They are for showing too. It's hard to get it exactly right, but it's also hard to know what someone is truly feeling sometimes.

I focus on the curve and shape of the brown paint for so long that my own eyes blur. My stomach growls as I wash the paintbrushes. This painting is going to take some time.

*

It's easier to ignore their eyes when I've just spent all morning focusing on them. I politely return their smiles and gratefully accept the extra portion of food.

"If I didn't know any better, I'd think they were fattening you up for slaughter." Jillian eyes my tray distrustfully.

"It sure feels like that," I smirk. "Pass the salt, please."

*

"Good morning ladies," Sister Auburn greets us as we come into the classroom. She claps a hand over her mouth to stifle a laugh when I walk past her desk.

"What's wrong?" I turn in confusion. The whole class pauses to look at me.

"Oh, it's nothing," she giggles. "You just have some paint on your dress."

The amusement on the students' faces quickly changes to embarrassment for me. My cheeks burn hot as I look to see the smear of paint on my side.

"My apologies," I rush to explain, "I didn't notice. I'll go change right now."

"Oh goodness no," she reassures me. "There is no need to worry. I actually think it's very adorable, but we might need to get you some type of apron to protect your whites. It'd be a nightmare trying to get a stain like that out."

"Her whites?" Jillian arches an eyebrow. By the looks on the faces of the rest of the class, they want this answer too.

"Why yes." Sister Auburn smiles. "Everyone here will earn their whites one day. I was actually going to discuss this later, but I think this is the perfect introduction. Please take your seats and we'll get started."

"Now some of this will be repetitive for some of you. Bear with me while I run through the details for our newer citizens-in-training." Sister Auburn stands at the front of the room. Her delicate features don't distract from the powerful stance she now holds. She was born for the role of teaching.

"Earning your whites is a time-honored tradition passed down from records in a time before our own. Although it is said that the original mother wore white when she called for peace, we now know this to be more myth than fact. Nevertheless, white is a sacred color. Women wore it on their wedding days as it was thought to symbolize purity. All citizens must now earn the right to wear white as a symbol of pure hearts and marriage to the community. Our society is strong because we have this mindset. And as you are well aware, you've all been rescued and given the chance to live peacefully beside us."

Jillian rolls her eyes and I have to force myself not to smile.

"Some of you will earn your whites faster than others," Sister Auburn continues. Chairs shift as the class moves anxiously forward, hanging on her every word.

"This is not a competition. There are many things to take into consideration when being awarded your new role in life. Just like the graduates of our schools, you must have a certain degree of education. In addition to this, your contribution to society will be measured and graded. Last, but certainly not least, your purity of heart shown through acts of self service and peaceful cooperation will go far in determining your ceremony date."

Basically, I need to prove I can paint. I turn to stare out the window, watching the barren branches sway in the breeze that dances through the courtyard.

"The great news is that I have absolute faith that every single one of you will earn your whites one day."

"Except me," Jillian mutters under her breath. I turn to see Sister Auburn watching me intently.

"All of us will." I place a reassuring hand on Jillian's shoulder. Sister Auburn nods, pleased, and continues to instruct us on the ways of this insane world.

*

If we earn our whites, we'll be given our own single dwelling residence. We can choose to attend the university to further our education or continue working in our chosen field. We'll be allowed to marry whoever we want, all our needs will be provided for, and we can even attend high council meetings to vote if we desire.

The last part sticks with me. When Sister Auburn begins the reading lesson, I sneak out and head to the library.

The basic premise of voting in their system sounds simple enough but I would need many more of me, and many Mothers, to make a difference. I wonder if I can convince others to vote on changing things. Maybe they would if I can show them that their notions of what it means to be a savage are wrong.

I stay too long with the books, devouring their laws of voting, when I should really be painting. It seems so odd to have to force myself to do something that I love. When the subject matter becomes too dry to stomach any longer, I put the books away.

Despite my hesitation, the brush in my hand feels like coming home. I decide to focus on the background instead because it's easier to get lost in it that way. I tell myself that this isn't a good idea, it's not something they will want to see. But there's no way I could stay true to myself and neglect this vital part.

"It's just the background," I whisper to no one.

The ocean crashing against the rocks sends a spray of salty water into the air. Little droplets of moisture that cling to every bit of exposed skin. Like happy tears coming from the earth herself.

How many shades of blue can there be? Blue skies. Blue water. Deeper in the farthest depths, lighter where it is shallow. Whoever said blue is the color of sadness? That isn't true. Blue is the color of life.

I stand back to inspect the painting that isn't yet a painting in the fading light from the sunset, still unable to bring myself to switch on their false light. I'll see it like that when it's finished. For now, I need to see it my way.

The ocean was easy, comfortable even, although it was a tiny portion of the background. The real focus was on the rocks, but I'll have to add green tomorrow. It'll take me forever to get the landscape just right, but I'll get there.

I think I'll get there, I chuckle to myself as I clean the brushes in the mineral water. It's never taken me this long to complete a painting. But then again, the stakes have never been this high.

I've missed dinner. Actually, when the moon peeks through my blinds like it's trying to get a glimpse of what I've done I realize I've lost the rest of the day in this room. I debate on heading to the cafeteria anyway to see if they have anything left. I'm sure they would, but I'm really not that hungry. Painting fuels me in an unexplainable way.

I turn the canvas so I can't see it. The thought of something unfinished staring back at me all night will keep me awake. Then I nestle myself into the soft and warm blankets as a dreamless, gloriously dreamless, and peaceful sleep carries me away.

✝ CHAPTER TEN ✝

There's a sudden knock at my door which almost causes me to swipe the black paint across the canvas. Thankfully, I have a steady hand.

"Who is it?" I call out, angry at the intrusion. I almost had this line perfect and now I'll need to stop.

The tray of half-eaten food stares back at me from the corner of the bed. I honestly can't remember them delivering it. Maybe it's time for the next one.

The door handle rattles as Jillian's voice calls from the other side, "Are you going to let me in?"

"Hang on." Reluctantly, I drop the paintbrush in the jar of mineral water and hurry to clean up the forgotten food before tidying up my bed. The paint on my hand leaves a smear on the clean pillowcase. I give up.

The door swings open to reveal Jillian standing with her arms folded over her chest staring at me like I have two heads. I blink as the harsh light of the hall temporarily blinds me. *How long has it been since I've seen it?*

"This isn't healthy," Jillian scolds. "You need to leave your room."

How long have I been in here? Hours? Days? It feels like I just woke up. "What time is it?"

"Gods, Brooke." Jillian pushes past me into the room and stares at the mess. I step in front of her, embarrassed, but she's already seen it.

"I don't care what they say. This isn't good for you. I'm not going to let you wither away in here while they all wait anxiously to see what entertainment you'll provide for their boring lives." Her eyes narrow. "You need to get some fresh air."

"The window is open." I shrug.

"Did you do this when you'd paint back home?" She's trying to understand something that even I don't understand. "Did you lock yourself up for weeks in a dark room?"

Weeks. I cringe at the word. "I've never had that kind of time before."

"Well, you might as well let me see it," she sighs. "I want to know what caused you to disappear."

"It's not done." Anxiety makes my heart race.

"How much longer then?" she asks.

"Soon," I promise, wishing she would leave.

"Not good enough." She shakes her head. "I'm not one of those awestruck mothers dressed in white tiptoeing past your door. You need to take a break. Come outside for a walk with me."

"I can't yet." She waits for me to explain, but how can I tell her that their eyes watching me and waiting for me to impress them is more than I can stand? I'd rather just finish this and then come out. They can judge me then.

"I'm not leaving until you tell me when you are going to come out of this room." Jillian plants her feet firmly on the carpet. I glance at the window. The late afternoon sun stares back at me. The tray must have been from lunch.

"I'll finish it tonight," I promise. "But I have to work on it now."

"Tonight." Jillian nods. "I'll come get you in the morning."

*

Honestly, it's done. I just keep tweaking lines here and there. I've never focused so hard on a single painting. The rational side of my brain tells me it is good enough. But I want it to be better than good enough. Maybe I should have let Jillian see it. She would tell me to leave it alone. But what if she hated it? *What if they all hate it?*

By the light of the setting sun, I make a final decision to add the soft hues of lilac and rosewood instead of the brighter flowers I'd planned on. These remind me of the dried flowers sitting on the café tables in town.

It has to be good enough. The moon begins to rise, filling the room with a soft glow and illuminating the now finished canvas for a final time. I sit heavily on the bed and wrap the blanket around me. The painting looks exactly as I'd imagined it. This has to be good enough. I couldn't do any better than this.

*

I haven't kept my hands very clean and now the stains of the paint have dyed the crevices around my nails. Scrubbing hard enough to make my skin raw does nothing to make them go away. I sigh, wrapping my wet hair up in the soft towel, as I make my way to the wardrobe to find a dress not splattered with paint. This will have to be good enough too.

Jillian knocks on the door just as I finish drying my hair.

"It's open," I call out.

"Thank the gods." She smiles when she sees me. "You look like a real person again."

"Stop it." I roll my eyes. "We both know I had to get this done."

"Can I see it now?" Jillian's eyes dart to the back of the canvas. The painting itself faces the window.

"Might as well get this over with." I refused to look at it this morning. What's done is done. There's no going back now.

Jillian gasps as she stands beside me. I knew she would do that.

"That bad?" I nudge her playfully.

"Brooke, it's amazing. They are going to throw those damn white clothes at you." Her eyes never leave the painting.

"That was the plan, right?" I sigh. "What am I supposed to do with it? Do I just carry it outside and display it somewhere?" The memory of standing on the wharf in the middle of the crowd while painting the lines of my father's machine haunts me. For a moment it was beautiful, and then my whole world changed.

"What do you want to do with it?" she asks.

"I want to burn it."

She peels her eyes away from the art and turns to glare at me. "We should set it up in the entrance room of the dome. If you keep it in here, you'll have throngs of people filtering in and out of your space."

"Let's do that." I nod in agreement. "Both me and her need to get out of this room anyway."

Jillian's gaze drifts back to the canvas. "She looks just like your sister."

"But she isn't really." I wink. "That's the original mother rising up through the ashes and bringing peace to the land. She is all of us."

"Oh, but of course," Jillian plays along solemnly. "They are going to drool over this. Thank goodness you are here."

*

My painting, *their painting,* sits in the middle of the entrance room to the welcome center. Citizens come from all over the city to see the spectacle. I feel less like the celebrity Rosemary and Charlotte proclaim me to be and more like a freak of nature. My head stays lowered and my footsteps are light as I walk. I take every compliment as humbly as I can, even as pride swells inside of me.

Then Mother Wolfe learns that the Council of the Arts wants to see me.

There's a flurry of activity when I'm given new gray dresses- *not white yet, but that would be rude of me to bring this up-* and Mother Wolfe sits me down to pleat my hair.

The Council of the Arts consists of two ancient Mothers with distant eyes and creaky bones. I'm worried they will turn to dust as they sit at the table across from me. They smell as old as the books that surround us in the library.

"It's been many years since we've had a young artist of your caliber," one of the women croaks. When she bends to take a sip of her tea, the other woman picks up her sentence, "We'd like to take the painting on a traveling tour through the district. At the end, it will be brought home to the Fine Arts Museum."

I nod, even though this doesn't seem like a question they want me to answer. A small pang of worry tenses my shoulders. Why does it need to travel? What if they damage it? *It isn't mine,* I remind myself. *I painted it for them.*

"We want you to attend the university near the mountains. The arts program there is struggling to find new talent. But you'll be in the company of the professors, some of the greatest artists of our time." I don't know which woman speaks. They both seem to have the same voice.

But I do know the thought of meeting other painters excites me. I fold my hands softly in my lap, careful not to let it show. It feels wrong to feel this happy right now.

*

Sister Auburn waits for me outside the library and she is practically bouncing from joy. She simply becomes Charlotte as she wraps her arms around me. Her hug is so warm it reminds me of Meghan.

Meghan. I want to see my sister one last time before she begins her journey around their world.

"I knew you could do it," Charlotte whispers in my ear before Mother Wolfe calls for her.

I quietly slip away down the empty hall, hurrying to the entrance of the Welcome Center where my painting sits on display. Curators are already bringing in the glass frame that the painting will travel in.

"Can I have a moment?" I place my hand gently on one man's shoulder. His eyes light up in stunned recognition and he nods as he backs away, pulling the other man along with him.

Alone with my painting, I trail a finger along the curved outline of my sister's cheek. But she isn't my sister, she's the representation of the original mother who these people seem to worship. A crown of dried wildflowers on her head. A swollen, pregnant belly stretching the seams of her flowing white dress. Meghan would laugh at me if I showed her this. I guess it's my own private joke.

"I thought you wanted to burn it," Jillian chuckles beside me. I didn't hear her walk up.

"It served its purpose, I guess." I take one last look before turning away. "I just wanted to say goodbye."

*

The citizen ceremony is small and uneventful. After everything I've been through, I assumed there would be some kind of grand celebration. I am allowed to invite whoever I want though.

Jillian stands next to Peter near the barren willow tree. They've been spending a lot of time together. It felt wrong not to ask him to come. Rosemary and Charlotte are by my side. I thought about inviting Calder, but the look on Mother Auburn's face as she stands with her thin arms folded over her chest tells me I made the right decision. I didn't invite her, but they needed three Mothers' blessings for the ceremony and apparently, she decided to come.

Mother Wolfe is just as proud as can be. She acts like this is partially her doing. Mother Neil gives her blessings freely. Her husband Charles isn't here. I haven't seen him since the walk in the fields. Mother Auburn seems resigned, making sure I hear the seriousness in her voice, before Rosemary- *now my sister*- is allowed to hand me the cloth package containing a white robe tied up tight with a satin bow.

Then it's done. It's all over. All the work, all this stress, all this time spent so that I can get a new damn dress.

*

Mother Auburn stops me in the hall and waves the other girls forward. Charlotte lingers uncertainly until her mother gives a stern look which makes her head hang down and her feet start moving. My heart hammers against my chest, but I will myself to stand still and keep my composure.

"You may not fully be the barbarian I thought you were," Mother Auburn states. *Is this her way of apologizing?* "But nothing you are doing is fooling me."

Nope. I bite my lip and listen to her words, hoping they won't be as harsh as it feels like they are going to be.

"The Mothers think that any rational and caring woman would do whatever it takes to try and save the world so they don't fault you for this. In fact, they think that makes you worthy," she continues. "I do not agree. You are not as smart as you think you are. We've all been watching you since you arrived. The Mothers eyes are everywhere, especially in the Welcome Center. You should also return the books you read to their proper places. Yes, voting is the right way to change the system, but this system is in place for a reason and no amount of effort on your part is going to change that."

I feel like she slapped me across the face with just her words and they weren't even that bad. I say nothing, even though there are many words I want to use too. She isn't finished insulting me yet.

"I know you don't want to be here, that you despise us for having what you did not, and for that reason alone I don't trust you. The other Mothers are too kind. They don't realize dangerous snakes hide in the shadows." Mother Auburn's eyes flick down to the package held tightly in my hand. "But you did your part to earn those whites. Don't make me regret my blessing."

I stand shocked as she storms past me and breathe deeply, willing my heart rate to return to normal. *Was that last part an insult or a compliment?* That woman is really hard to read. Thankfully, I don't need her blessing to understand my purpose. I'll never stop trying to right the wrongs of this world no matter how long I live.

All she did was add fuel to the fire.

✝ CHAPTER ELEVEN ✝

I've started walking the paths in the empty field outside the city every day. It's amazing how much room there is to walk. I don't think I'm ever going to get tired of this. The chilling breeze doesn't bother me as much now that I can wear a white sweater made from wool. Charlotte gave it to me as a gift.

The girls want to take me shopping this weekend. I get to choose from a wide variety of differently styled white clothes now, unlike the limited variety of unshapely gray dresses and pants. *Perks of being a citizen.*

Then, next week, I'll pack up everything I own and board the energy efficient train that travels through the district which will take me seventy-five miles to the university in the mountains. Charlotte tells me not to be nervous, we can still see each other on weekends, but I'm not worried about that. *Okay, this train thing makes me a little nervous.* The thought of meeting the artists, no matter how old they are, fills me with a secret happiness.

Jillian has been distant these past few days. There is a bitter jealousy in her tone but she won't tell me why. I don't understand it, this was her plan after all, but maybe she just doesn't want me to leave. It's too late for that now. I'm ready to go. It's not like I have another option anyway.

The only thing still bothering me is not being able to tell Calder goodbye. Rosemary tells me he is doing better. It's her own little game, giving me updates like a spy in the historical fiction novels I've just started reading. She thinks we have a secret love affair and no amount of my denial will convince her of the truth. It's nice to hear how he is doing though.

I glance over my shoulder at the hospital dome in the distance before I take the worn dirt path down the hill that dips into the valley with a crystal-clear lake. The water is fresh, I've already tasted it, and as icy cold as the ocean.

The path loops around the lake, sloping over rocks and exposed roots and ducking under tree branches that form a thorny brown canopy against the blue skies. This place will be beautiful come spring I'm told. Maybe one day I'll see it. More likely it will be like everything else I've left behind, just another memory I can paint.

The earth crunches behind me and I freeze like a rabbit unsure of which direction to take. No one usually comes out here, and the only other person who has ever followed me on the empty paths is Charles. He wouldn't be able to navigate this terrain with his cane.

Another crunch, the sound grows louder as the snap of a branch connects with heavy boots. A chill creeps up my spine, raising goosebumps on my neck and pulsating unexpected warmth through my core. I'd know that sound anywhere. A watchman's boots crashing through the underbrush. Not just any watchman either, a big, clumsy, thick skulled watchman. I don't even have to turn around. I can feel his presence there.

My heart beat quickens and I hide my joy behind a sarcastic smile. *Why am I acting this way?* It doesn't matter. I'll be gone next week.

"What are you doing out here?" I call back over my shoulder. "I thought you must have forgotten how to walk with how much time you spent just laying around in that bed."

"Brooke," he says my name softly as he steps into the clearing, but when I turn to see him my smile falters. His face is hard, his jawline set, and his eyes are fixed on the lake behind me. He's no longer Calder. He's once again a watchman. "I need my map back."

"What map?" I cross my arms over my chest, feeling the paper crease against my skin. I still keep it with me always even though I can find this information in the books. I'm hesitant to give it up now.

"I don't have time for these games," he says coldly. "It's a required part of my gear. I need it back now."

Why does his tone hurt so much? It doesn't hurt. I'm being ridiculous. Calder was never anything more than a watchman. But I don't understand, "Gear? What do you mean, gear?"

He doesn't skip a beat. It's as if he already anticipated this question. More than I care to admit, he is his mother's son. "They went out to retrieve my gear after you brought me in. I have everything except the map. I have to report back to my unit and they'll demote me if I'm missing pieces."

Unit? Missing pieces? The words swirl around me as foreign as the day I arrived in this crazy world. But I refuse to be naive anymore. "They'll demote you to what? Something less than you are right now?"

He lowers his eyes so I can't see his reaction, but the moment is fleeting and I feel awful for saying anything. I know enough now to understand that the watchmen are lesser than the average citizen. But my people are even lower than that. *My people.* Am I even with them anymore? I stare down at the fibers of the white wool sweater.

"I just need the map, Brooke. And then I'll leave you alone." He's so deflated. "Please give it to me."

I refuse to believe that the reason I lived in fear for months outside the wall now grovels for a piece of paper. This is insane. *Why is he acting this way?*

"Fine." I raise my chin. "I'll tell you where the map is if you tell me why you've changed. Why are you so eager to return to the watchmen when you were so happy here?" I'm proud of the strength in my voice. It echoes through the lifeless valley. I'm not hurt. I refuse to let this hurt me. I just want to know the truth.

"It's nothing to worry about." His eyes shift as he avoids my real question, and the watchman's stare looks every place but to where my own two feet stand firmly. "It's just time to return to my unit."

"You can't go now!" The words rush from my lips and I take a deep breath to stop more from falling out that sound this desperate. "You've been seriously injured. You need more time to heal."

"I don't have time." He grits his teeth. "I need to go now."

"Why now?" I force my voice to remain soft instead of screaming. "They have to understand that you got hurt."

"They need me," he states. "And I need my map."

"I don't want to give it to you." It's an honest answer, I've been short on those these days.

"You have to." He steps forward, closing the distance between us. "I can't handle any more problems right now."

"Fine." I glare at him, my own jaw clenched. He's not my problem either. "Just explain to me why you need to go back. I can tell you are lying about something."

He runs his fingers through his hair, it's grown longer over the past few weeks, and contemplates the words he wants to say before giving in. "I lied to you about Endre," he whispers.

"You what?" I take a step back, horrified. Whatever fear shows on my face is enough to break this trance. He flinches as if I punched him in the gut.

"I didn't mean to lie," he continues as the watchman's face slips away and the Calder I knew for a brief moment returns. "I thought I understood what was happening, but it's so much bigger than I imagined. There's been more situations, more unexplained deaths, all from boats drifting away from the cities on their own. They say a war is coming. I need to be there for my friends."

"A war with who?" It's a painful whisper. Images from the texts I've read explaining wars of the past show like paintings in my mind. I know the word. *But how? Why?*

"I don't know exactly." Calder rubs his hand across the back of his neck. "We aren't the only landmass in the world. It makes sense that others would have survived the rising seas. Maybe they've depleted their land and come to take from us."

I stagger back, gripping the rough bark of the tree behind me. This is too much to take in at once. "Other people? Other societies? They crossed the ocean to attack us?"

"Why wouldn't they?" Calder asks, studying the clear water of the lake beside us. "We did our part protecting this land from overuse. Maybe others weren't so lucky."

"Lucky?" My jaw drops. "My people live outside the walls, cut off from all of this, while your people lie to them and hoard the earth for themselves."

He shakes his head, a smile on his lips, as his eyes travel slowly down my body. "Those aren't your people anymore," he smirks. "I shouldn't have done it, shouldn't have risked everything for a hot-headed artist, but I did and I don't have any regrets. These are your people now too. I've given you a better life."

I can't even process his words right now, too many of them are swirling around in my head. *Oh gods, outside the walls.*

"They'll attack outside of the walls first. My family is in danger." I clasp my hands over my mouth to stop from crying out.

"Not if we meet them out to sea." A steely resolve hardens his face. "I need the map. I need to rejoin my unit. And I promise you I'll do my best to keep everyone safe."

A deep fear settles in the pit of my stomach. "You can't go. You promised me you'd try to understand and change things here." Even as I stutter these words, I know they are meaningless right now.

"This is bigger than us." He avoids looking me in the eyes. "I don't have time to do anything else but fight to protect the wall. I'm a watchman. This is my job. Now tell me where the map is so that I can go back."

I don't want him to leave. No matter how thick skulled he is, I don't want him to get hurt again. But I don't want my family to get hurt either. Hot tears well in my eyes as I reach into my shirt and pull out the piece of paper. Calder's face lights up in amusement. His playful smile shatters my heart and at the same time, it makes me want to smack him. I giggle as the tears roll down my face. *Hitting a watchman is a bad idea.*

"Thanks for keeping it warm," he sighs in relief. The pad of his thumb brushes against my knuckles as he slides the map out of my hand. The instant we touch he looks up at me, staring deeply into my eyes. His eyes are glossy too, the deep brown moistened by unshed tears.

"I heard about your painting," he whispers. "They said you were amazing, but I already knew that. Have fun at the university. Maybe I'll see you again one day."

He gives me a broken smile and turns to leave. His heavy boots crunch the thick clots of dirt as he walks. With every step, my heart breaks again, snapping like broken branches under his feet. I wipe a hand angrily across my face, willing the tears to stop. This is all too much to take in. *How can this be happening?*

"Calder wait!" I didn't mean to cry out but my shattering heart betrayed me. He groans painfully as he turns to the sound of my voice.

In half a breath, he's crossed the clearing and pulled me into his arms. I don't breathe anymore. His eyes are pleading as he looks down into mine and his warm, calloused hand finds its place at the base of my neck, his fingers tangling in my hair. A painful lump forms in my chest as my heart tries to put itself together too fast.

And then his lips are on mine. Rough, demanding, needing. I gasp, trying to breathe in some air to cool down the fire on my skin. He pulls away just enough so that our lips still touch and the breath I take is his.

He's waiting for me to kiss him back and I know he'll leave if I don't. *Maybe I am a barbarian.* There is no other reason why I let my body take over my mind. I should push him away. *This is wrong.* I wrap my arms around his shoulders, pulling him closer to me, and force his lips apart with mine, hungrily returning the kiss. He tastes like earth. Strong and rich and comforting. I drink him in like he's water.

I don't cry when he breaks away, but every part of me wants to. His whole body shakes with ragged breaths as he rests his forehead against mine. With my eyes still closed, I feel droplets of moisture drip from his face to my cheek.

"I have to go now." His voice is hoarse. I nod, not trusting myself to speak. My eyes stay closed as I listen to the sound of his boots walking away. When I can no longer hear him, I let myself crumple at the base of the tree.

*

I don't know how long I sit in the dirt. My new white dress must be stained by now. A brown squirrel scurries across the path, pausing to look up at me curiously. I want to laugh, but only a choked sob comes out. The frightened squirrel skitters up a tree getting as far away from me as he can.

Despite the stinging cold of my cheek, my lips still feel warm and I can't bring myself to touch them. I don't want to wipe the taste away. *Oh gods, I kissed a watchman.* I'm almost disgusted with myself. I want to taste him again.

Forcing these foreign thoughts deep down where I hope I can't reach them, I make myself stand and start to walk. The watchmen didn't kill Endre. My family isn't safe. There are people coming to attack us. These are the things I should be worrying about and yet, *I might never see Calder again.*

I pull the wool sweater closer around me, clutching at my betrayal of a heart. Just when I thought I knew who I was I realize I can't even trust myself. *Why did I call him back?* He seemed so fragile and broken even as his strong arms held me against him. A yearning ache pulls at my chest. I don't want him to go. *Could his mother do something?* Now my thoughts are just as irrational as my impulses are.

My family is in danger. A war is coming. Calder promised to keep them safe. What about his family? How will they take the news that he is going to fight? *Charlotte.* I owe it to Calder to make sure his sister is okay.

*

The world is different when I arrive back in the city. Heads are turned down, faces lost in silent contemplation, instead of beaming with cordial smiles. I brush past a woman holding a small child's hand, the boy dragging his feet as she pulls him along. She jumps out of the way startled and murmuring apologies.

I almost stop to ask her what's wrong, but I catch sight of Charles hobbling across the street. He waves to me. I wish I hadn't noticed. *Would it be rude to run away?* Charlotte's dome is just behind the school. I haven't been there yet, but she pointed it out to me. If I take the side street now, I can avoid Charles altogether.

"Brooke," he calls out. "I've been looking for you."

Curse the gods. I hesitate, giving him enough time to catch up.

"I'm glad to run into you," he puffs with labored breaths. "I was just about to check again at the Welcome Center."

"Why are you looking for me?" My eyes go everywhere but to his face. I just want to see Charlotte right now.

"The man I told you about is here," Charles smiles. "The circumstances aren't good. He's in town for the emergency council meeting tonight. But I'd like to arrange a lunch tomorrow if you are free."

"Sure," I say quickly, hoping he'll take the hint and leave. "I'll meet you at the café on Main Street. But if you'll excuse me, I have somewhere I need to be."

"Of course." He nods and lets me pass.

I rush down the street and cross the road to the sidewalk that leads to the single residence domes. *Why did I just agree to that?* It's another question I can't answer. My brain is somewhere outside of my head right now. Let me just check on Charlotte and I'll deal with Charles tomorrow.

*

Charlotte looks just like I feel. Her eyes are red and swollen from crying. She breaks down when she sees me standing at the door and I hold her upright as I maneuver us to the sofa, letting her cling to my arm as she sobs.

"Can I get you something?" I ask once she's seated.

She points to the back room behind the partition that looks like a kitchen and croaks out between tears, "I was trying to make tea."

Her house is neat and tidy, everything tucked securely into place. Except the broken cup in the sink and the tea leaves strewn about the counter. I hurry to clean them both up and then search the cabinets until I find a new teacup. I'm not exactly sure how to make tea, but I've read about it and the process seems easy. I scoop the loose leaves into the cup and pour boiling water over them.

The steam smells good enough as I carry the mug back into her living room. She's pulled the large knit blanket from the back of the chair and wrapped herself up in it.

"Did you hear already?" she asks. The words set off a fresh wave of tears. "I can't believe this is happening to us. We've never hurt anyone or done anything wrong. And my little brother has to go fight them."

I swallow rocks as I sit beside her not wanting to speak and make her pain any worse.

"It's just too much," she continues to cry. "This is what the mother warned us about. She knew how violent people could be. They don't deserve this land, not after everything we've done to protect it."

"Are you going to the meeting tonight?" I have to say something to change the subject before the wrong thing slips from my lips.

"I suppose I have to," she sighs as she reaches for the cup.

"Can I come too?" I shyly ask.

"Of course," she nods as she blows against the steam. "All citizens are allowed to attend."

I watch her take a sip of the tea, hoping I made it right. Her grimace causes me to laugh uncontrollably as my own tears stream down my face. "Is it that bad?"

The laughter is infectious. She giggles through her heartbreak, "Oh Brooke, I'm so glad you are here."

☦ CHAPTER TWELVE ☦

Neither of us feel like eating, but Charlotte teaches me how to make tea and we do our best to pass the time in the evening until the meeting starts. The City Hall dome is on the other end of the city. We take Charlotte's single bike to get there. I grip tightly to her waist as she stands and pedals. Yet another thing I have to learn to do- how to ride a bike.

She reassures me that not everyone knows how. The carts are attached to a bike like contraption. The principal is the same, but you don't fall over when you stop. They are much easier to handle. Still, I add this new skill to my list of things I want to do. I like how fast it moves.

It seems the entire city is trying to get into the building when we arrive. A line forms as everyone waits to enter but the usual smiles are gone. I can just imagine how hard this must be for them. Knowing the world isn't what it seems and there are people who want to hurt you. It takes a lot of effort not to roll my eyes.

Charlotte has to sit up front near the other mothers-in-training. Thankfully, I spot Rosemary in the crowd sitting next to Paige and she waves me over while holding a seat for me.

"Where's Maisy?" I ask looking back over my shoulder.

"She's not coming." Paige dabs a cloth against her eyes. "The news was too much for her to take. Her mother came over to be with her."

"It's hard for all of us," Rosemary sighs as she reaches for my hand. "How are you doing? Did Calder find you and say goodbye? I told him where you usually walk."

Hearing his name makes this newfound ache cut a little deeper. I nod and lick my lips, but the taste is gone- replaced by the sweetness of herbal tea. I'll probably never get the taste back. I blink hard to stop myself from crying and turn to look around the room. Everyone here must think I'm just as upset as they are, but my reasons are my own.

The City Hall dome is huge, it's almost as big as the Welcome Center, but unlike the other buildings there are no straight walls inserted to divide the space. Instead, rows of circular step benches curve around the entire dome and slope almost to the top. The men who stand in the back rows could reach up to touch the ceiling.

I quickly scan the crowd around and below me. There are no men seated with the women. They stand along the top perimeter and cluster around the exits as if forming a human wall of protection against the outside world.

Looking at them breaks my heart, so I focus on the empty seats in the center of the room. Forty chairs that I can count. Since I don't see Mother Auburn anywhere, I assume these seats are reserved for the council. But they are arranged in a circle facing each other instead of the crowd.

My investigation is cut short when one of the mothers-in-training seated near Charlotte stands. Her voice echoes through the room electronically, "Sisters and Brothers, please quiet down. The Mothers are coming now."

Mother Auburn walks in first with her head held high as a row of Mother's wearing white silk robes trails in behind her. They take the open seats facing one another and when the last Mother sits, Mother Auburn leans forward to address them. Her voice is also amplified. The entire situation feels unreal, as if we are all eavesdropping on a conversation between the Mothers. Everyone stays silent, holding their breath, and hanging on their every word like children hiding behind a door listening to their parents.

"What do we know about these ships?" a Mother asks.

"Only that they've been increasing the number of deaths of those who drift too far out to sea," Mother Auburn states.

"Well, that's not our problem," another Mother interjects. I clench my teeth as she speaks.

"No." Mother Neil shakes her head. "It wasn't our problem, but the increase in reports tells us that this is some type of warning and the distance these boats have drifted is lessening. This means that whoever is out there is coming closer."

The women around me sniffle and cough softly, trying their best to keep their cries silent.

"Do we know who they are or what they want?" the only Mother with a shaved head asks.

"Not without approaching them," the Mother seated next to her explains. "And we've already seen what happens with that."

The youngest Mother in the group sighs. "Couldn't we just send a small convoy out to speak with them?"

"How many watchmen are you willing to risk?" Mother Neil asks calmly. I turn to look at the faces of the men, but they don't look anymore distraught upon hearing this question.

"Honestly?" the young Mother continues. "Why don't we just get the barbarians to do it?"

As often as I've heard this term spoken, it shouldn't insult me as much as it does now.

"The barbarians are no use to us." Mother Auburn glances up and it seems her eyes lock onto mine, which can't be possible. How would she be able to spot me in this sea of faces? "They refuse to help.

They refuse to fight. They say it is the watchmen's job to protect the wall."

A collective murmur ripples through the crowd. Despite the utter outrage on their faces which makes me sink down deeper into my seat, a small burning ember of pride burns in my chest for my people. *They are refusing because they are tired of the way they've been treated.*

"They have to fight," the young Mother exclaims. "Do they not care about protecting their homes?"

"Savages don't care about anything, you know this," a Mother chimes in. "But maybe we can force them somehow." My heart beats loudly and I struggle to breathe as the tension in the room rises.

"Those barbarians are nothing but trouble. They are not our problem."

"Maybe we should just seal the gates and leave them outside like we had to do with the Cortez Gate."

"It's a manning issue keeping them open for their children anyway. My mother argued against this policy."

"Close the gates and let them deal with the hostiles by themselves."

"There's not enough watchmen to man the entire wall and if we don't know how many hostiles there are then bringing them to our shores is a mistake."

"How would you know that?"

"Enough, Mothers. Let's discuss this calmly." Mother Auburn places her hands together under her chin. "I asked Atlas to join us tonight for just this reason. I know we don't normally ask men to speak, but these are special circumstances and he is the commander of the watchmen. He deals with violence on a daily basis so his knowledge is valuable to this discussion. And if we vote to direct efforts against the invading hostiles, then Atlas will be spearheading this campaign under our approval."

She directs her attention to the back of the room. "Atlas, will you come forward please?"

I don't know how I didn't see the watchman dressed in green when I scanned the crowd, but I remember how good they are at hiding in the shadows. This watchman is aged and worn, his salt and pepper hair cut closely to his head, and a long scar running up his cheek. But he doesn't carry himself as if he were old. His barrel chest and hardened muscles are distinguishable even through the uniform. It's only the way he favors one knee over the other that reflects any sign of frailty.

Some of the Mothers shift in their seats, turning their heads up and smiling. He must have made an impression on them at some point, but he doesn't seem to notice as he stands in the center of their circle.

"What do you propose we do, Atlas?" Mother Wolfe asks a little too flirtatiously as she draws out his name.

"Thank you for the opportunity to speak." He addresses them all with a courteous nod. "As I've told Mother Auburn, I suggest that we bring the battle out to sea."

"Will you have the numbers needed to fight without the savages joining?" the Mother with a shaved head asks.

"No," he states flatly. "But we will recruit more of our men who have ended their contracts with the watch. This will have to be enough."

"I vote that we just close the gates and focus on protecting the wall from the inside," the young Mother cries out as she twists the wedding band on her finger. "This is madness. What if you all die out there on the ships?"

"We are going to have to shut the gates regardless," Mother Neil sighs. "Without enough watchmen left to stand guard, the gates will be too vulnerable to intrusion."

"We should have already done it," another Mother states. "Seal them off now it'll be less to worry about."

"I agree," a third Mother pipes in. "If they won't fight to protect it then they don't deserve the land."

Zander. They are going to take away Zander's childhood.

"Let me convince them to fight with you!"

It's not courage that forces me to stand, it's pure animalistic panic. *They can't take the earth away from Zander.*

Rosemary gasps, pulling at my arm. "Brooke," she cries. "Sit down."

My voice wasn't as loud as their electronic projections, but the whole room turns to look at me anyway. Mother Auburn's eyes shoot daggers into my soul, but I ignore her. She's not the one I'm speaking to.

"I promise I can convince the people outside the walls to stand with you against the hostiles. Just give me a chance to prove it." I push Rosemary's fingers off my arm and give her a sad smile. "I have to do this," I whisper before walking down the steps.

All of the eyes in the room follow my descent. I feel judged, like an ancient painting displayed in the Fine Arts Museum. But I hold my head high as I address the Mothers in the center of the room.

"Please," I beg. "You've done so much for me. I at least have to try and help." My eyes brush across Atlas' face. The strong watchman suddenly looks pale as he stares at me with mouth agape. I don't have time to wonder about his expression.

"How can you help?" Mother Neil asks gently. "We've already reasoned with them and they refused."

Mother Wolfe smiles with proud tears in her eyes as she turns to the women sitting around her. "I've seen her do it. She has a way of convincing rebels to behave like civilized citizens. The way of the Mother is in her blood, how else would she be able to paint her so well? If Brooke says she can convince them, then I give her my full support."

The other Mothers look to one another. They may not know my name, but they've heard of my painting by now. This makes me a celebrity in their eyes, but instead of standing proud I humbly look at the floor and await their final judgement.

"Please let me help."

A roar of approving applause vibrates through the building. I glance over my shoulder to see Rosemary clapping despite the tears streaming down her cheeks.

"No." Mother Neil dabs at the corner of her eye to dry the tears as she speaks loudly into the microphone attached to her robes. "Brooke has already been through too much. We can't let any harm come to her. She deserves to live in peace here with us."

"I'll take care of her," Atlas' baritone voice echoes through the room.

"I'll do everything in my power to keep her safe and return her here to you," he continues once the room quiets down. "But this might save us all."

The votes of the Mothers are a loud spoken "yes" but apparently, they weren't loud enough.

"It's time for a recess," Mother Auburn declares as she stands from her seat. "We need a moment to process this new information. Sister Auburn." She casts a cold glare at her daughter. "Please escort our darling Brooke to my chambers immediately."

I can't bring myself to look at Mother Auburn. Dread pricks my skin all over and makes it hard to breathe. Charlotte takes my arm gently and the citizens in the room give me a standing ovation as I quietly exit the room.

"I can't believe you did that," Charlotte exclaims when the door shuts behind us. I was wrong. There are straight walls in this dome. A circular hall wraps around the building with doors leading to rooms built beneath the stairs.

"I'm sorry," I stammer as the anxiety catches up to me. "I wasn't thinking straight. I just wanted to do something to help."

"I don't want to lose you." She pulls me in for a hug. "But do you really think you can do it?"

Do I? I'm not sure. I know I can convince Tordon and maybe he can convince Aegir and after that...

"I think I can." I pull away from the embrace. "There really doesn't seem to be another choice."

"You really are amazing." She dries the tears on her cheeks with her sleeve. "I almost wish Calder did bring you home to marry. He'd be lucky to have you."

*

Mother Auburn's chambers sharply contrast to the simple tidiness of Charlotte's home. Rich red velvet lines dark wood furniture. There's a sofa in the corner that matches the two cushioned high back chairs that face the polished grand desk with ornamental knobs made of bronze. A burgundy rug interwoven with patterns of gold lines the floor. The room is clean but the colors are so loud and dark that it feels oppressive in here. Maybe that's why my hands are shaking. But the creak of the door opening behind me makes them shake more.

"Leave us," Mother Auburn demands as she breezes into the room. Charlotte nods, giving me a reassuring smile despite my eyes begging her not to go.

"Take a seat," Mother Auburn states as she leans against the desk with her arms crossed. I choose the second chair, the one furthest away from her, so she can't hear the pounding of my heart.

"You may have them all fooled, but not me. I know what game you are playing. You think this is your ticket out of here. That you'll just get to run back to your rusted wharf and tell everyone their life is a lie." Her eyes burn holes in my skin as she speaks. "They won't believe you and even if some do, what good will it do them? You'll make an already hard existence that much harder. Sure, some will fight to get inside the wall, but I will never allow that. Those savages are no match for trained and armed watchmen. All you will do is bring destruction to them. My sole job is to protect the earth and I will never let anyone abuse it."

I want to speak, but my throat is dry, and it's not like she wants to hear what I have to say anyway.

"Damn Henry and his stupid program." She slaps her hand against the desk. "This is exactly what change brings."

"What program?" I ask, genuinely confused.

"To bring barbarians inside these walls," she smirks. "And not just the ones we need here or the sluts that get picked up by the watchmen, he wants to save them all. This is why men are no good at leading. The hero complex is too strong. But Henry is not in charge here, I am. And I refuse to let you damage our society."

I take a deep breath in, licking my lips. The ghost of Calder's kiss this morning gives me a quiet sort of strength against this woman.

"You're wrong," I say as firmly as I can. "I want to go to the university. I want to paint and meet others like me. There is no life for me outside the walls anymore. This is where I belong. But if I don't do my part to help, then how can I say that I do belong here? Isn't that what the Mother would have wanted? This is our society after all."

"Oh, you are good," Mother Auburn chuckles. "It always amazes me how people can be so blind to what's staring them in the face, but I guess when it comes in a pretty package it's easier to ignore the truth."

"I don't understand what you are saying." I lower my eyes and rub my hands on the soft material of my dress. "If you don't want my help that's alright, but offering was the right thing to do."

"It seems I no longer have a choice," she sighs. "The Mothers have already voted. You'll leave with Atlas tomorrow morning for the training station at Inlet Bay." My eyes light up but I keep them down turned, trying my hardest not to gloat.

"As you wish." I stand to leave. "Was there anything else you wanted to discuss?" She waves me away as she settles into the large arm chair behind the desk.

"One more thing," she calls out as I reach the door. "Does any of this have to do with my son being sent back to the watch?"

"Yes." I turn to face her, taking the slightest bit of pleasure from the way she seems to momentarily falter. She wasn't expecting the truth. "But not in the way you are implying. I want to protect him just like I want to protect all of us. It's what the Mother would have wanted."

*

Charlotte is waiting outside the door. She's all smiles as she laces her arm through mine. I fight to keep a solemn face.

Even as I'm led through the main room- the meeting has been postponed but the crowd still lingers- and even as they begin to cheer, thanking me for being their savior, I fight to keep the excitement at bay.

I catch a glimpse of the watchman named Atlas as I'm swept against the tide of well-wishers. He studies me with a watchman's intensity, but even that can't stop the happy fish swimming and dancing inside my stomach. Rosemary and Paige squeal in delight as they push their way through the crowd to me. I allot them a simple smile, nothing more.

Outside, the chill night air dances around us. Mother Wolfe offers me a ride back to the Welcome Center in her cart. She smiles proudly as she pats my back when the people stop us to give one final word of gratitude.

As the cold wind whips my hair around my face in the back of the cart and cancels out the noise from the world, I wrap my arms around my body and clench my teeth to keep from laughing out loud. The thought I've worked so hard to suppress all evening now fills my entire being. *I am going home.*

☦ CHAPTER THIRTEEN ☦

"Jillian, wake up." I knock softly at her door. It's late at night and everyone in the Welcome Center is asleep. She regards me coolly, the same expression she has given the past few days. I ignore it as I walk into the room and sit on the bed while I wait for her to close the door.

"I'm going home," I whisper into her ear once she sits beside me.

Her eyes widen. "Brooke, we talked about this. They aren't going to let you run away, even if you are wearing white."

"No." I shake my head. "They are taking me outside the wall. There are other people, dangerous people, killing us off one by one and letting the unmanned boats crash back against the shores like they did to Endre. The watchmen are being sent to fight, but our people refuse to join. I'm going to convince them to help."

"Oh gods, Brooke," she gasps. "What are you doing? You are going to condemn our people to die. Let the watchmen do their job and leave us out of it."

I glance around the room. *Is it possible to hear us in here?* "You don't understand. There isn't another way. The watchmen need us."

"You're a traitor." She turns away from me. The word slices me in half. *Am I a traitor?*

There's so much I want to say, but I can't take the chance. I can only whisper and hope she understands, "I'll tell him for you."

*

Mother Wolfe knocked on my door just as the sun cracked the sky. Her eyes were already red rimmed from crying. My suitcases were sent to the waiting cart. Atlas was here to collect me.

Mercury stands outside the quiet cafeteria holding a basket of breakfast for me to take. "Atlas is a good man," he whispers, giving me a wink. "Don't worry about anything. He'll take care of you."

The early morning light has a golden glow that feels soothing as I step from the dimly lit dome. I blink as a trio of men come into focus. In the center of the group is the watchman named Atlas, his back is turned to me. I recognize Charles standing to the side, lost in conversation and clapping the watchman on the shoulder like they are long lost friends.

"It seems our lunch date turned to breakfast instead." Charles turns to smile at me. Something is different about him in this light and it isn't his newly bought glasses. I'd completely forgotten about lunch and it must show on my face.

"Never mind," Charles laughs. "This is the man I wanted you to meet."

Atlas looks over his shoulder. The intense stare he gave me last night is gone, replaced with distant and sad eyes. I don't know what has hurt this man so much, but I instantly want to make him smile. He reminds me of Calder in a way.

"Let's get going." Atlas moves over to the bike attached to the cart. The third man shakes Atlas' hand before walking alone down the sidewalk. I didn't get a chance to see his face. "We have a long journey ahead of us. The sooner we start, the sooner we get there."

I don't know what to say so I just climb into the back of the cart. The silent city, still asleep, begins to fade away as we travel. The large domes turn to boulders again. Maybe I should have requested more time. I didn't really get the chance to say goodbye to Charlotte and Rosemary. But then again, I wasn't able to say goodbye to everyone the first time my life completely shifted.

*

"Where are we going?" The further we get from the city, the more worried I become. This isn't the road I dragged Calder down. It's much too smooth. I'm not even sure where we are anymore. A moment of panic overwhelms me. I force myself to slow down and visualize the lines, remember the words, on Calder's map. *I shouldn't have given it to him.* I inhale deeply, pushing the thoughts away. Yesterday still hurts.

"When we get to the fields, we'll trade this cart for a pair of horses. Then it will be a few hours ride until we get to the Inlet Bay Shipyard," he calls back over his shoulder.

Maybe this is a better way, I think. Ships travel faster than walking. I'll get home sooner than I'd planned.

The road gets rougher and the cart bounces around. The back of Atlas' neck glistens with sweat.

"Why don't you let me pedal for a while?" I place my hand on his shoulder. His muscles tense as he stares straight ahead and I pull my hand back as if I'd burned him.

"No need," he states flatly. "We're stopping here."

I've seen pictures of horses in the textbooks, but I never imagined they'd be this big. I'm honestly terrified when Atlas takes the second saddle from the farmer who eyes me curiously.

"This is the artist," Atlas explains as he adjusts the straps under the belly of the beast. I stand a safe distance back as I smile at the man.

His jaw drops. "Well I'll be damned. Is this the one who's going to tame the barbarians?"

Atlas nods, taking the reins from the farmer and holding them out for me. My hands are slick so I press them against my back hoping they won't notice me drying them.

"I've never ridden a horse before," I explain. A playful humor lights up Atlas' eyes that takes years away from his face.

"Don't be nervous, sister." The farmer laughs. "Pegasus here is a gentle giant."

The only thing that gets me to put my foot in the stirrup and scramble ungracefully onto the horse's back is the thought of seeing my sister again. I shake as I grip the reins tightly, but it doesn't take any effort on my part for Pegasus to follow Atlas and the chestnut-colored beast he rides on. All I need to do is hang on.

After a while, the tension eases from my shoulders and I venture to rub my fingers through Pegasus' charcoal mane. He snorts, shaking his head abruptly, causing me to gasp out loud and put my hand back where it belongs. From up ahead I hear Atlas chuckle over the trotting of the horses' hooves.

We leave the main road and cut straight through the open fields. There's no sign of human life out here. No worn paths, no structures- I don't know how Atlas knows where to go.

Atlas slows down his horse so that she walks right beside Pegasus. I watch him out of the corner of my eye, waiting for him to speak. For some reason, I trust this watchman, but not enough to tell him what I'm thinking first. Apparently, he thinks the same thing.

We walk in silence for a while until he coughs to clear his throat. "You look just like her."

"My grandmother I'm assuming."

He nods and looks away.

"How did you know her?" I ask softly. This subject seems to cause him pain.

"I met her when your father was a baby. About a year after your grandfather passed away." There has to be so much more to the story. I wonder if I'll have to pry it from him as we move quietly through the fields for a while, the hooves of the horses creating a steady rhythm.

"What was she like?" I ask him. "I mean, what was she like when she was young?"

He smiles fondly at the memory. "Beautiful and stubbornly independent. She was smart and strong. A warrior. How did she die?"

"Her heart gave out with age," I explain gently. "I was a young child when it happened. During the sea burial we ate sugar kelp treats while dancing and singing to her on the deck of the boat. My father forbid us to cry, saying she'd want our laughter instead of tears."

"I'm glad for that." He swallows hard as he stares at the horizon. "She deserved to be surrounded by love."

It makes sense now. No man speaks about a woman that way, *unless*... "How long did you love her?"

"From the moment I heard her singing," he chuckles. "Maybe even before. And for the rest of my life after that."

"Did she love you too?" It's hard to picture my grandmother loving anyone but us. She'd always said the men in the city weren't her type when we teased her. I'd assumed she was heartbroken from the loss of my grandfather at such a young age, but maybe I was wrong.

"Probably not." Atlas stiffens in his saddle. "I promised myself I'd never bother her again. I was a coward when I was younger. I should have protected her, but then again, she didn't need my saving."

"A coward?" Everything about this watchman suggests hard years and battles won by strength. It's hard to see him as anything less than he is now.

"Oh yes." He smiles. "We can all be cowards. The trick is to fight to overcome it and be something more."

"So, did you do something more?" It's easy to talk to him, almost pleasant. I'd like to know his story.

"I'm still trying," he sighs. "But I might need your help."

"Me?" I laugh. "I mean, I guess I'm trying to do that now. But I'm not sure how good I'll be at it. I think I can convince at least one person to help and hopefully together we can convince more."

"Sometimes all it takes is one person, but don't worry about that now." He looks back over his shoulder and scans the fields as if he's worried someone is following us. But we'd see anyone coming from miles away out here. I arch an eyebrow as I wait for him to explain what he means.

"They already told me about you. I think you are exactly what we need," he states.

"Who told you? The Mothers?" I sigh. "They put too much faith in me, but like I said, I'll try."

"Not the Mothers, the men. Mercury and Todd radioed me weeks ago. They've been keeping an eye on you."

"Mercury is contacting you about me?" I think of his devilish winks and kindness. The day he gave me the salt. *Was it all some kind of trick?*

"Just reporting. He sends me messages sometimes. And when Todd heard you speaking that night at the bar, he told me you would be able to help."

"Help with what?" My heart begins to race. I knew the Mothers were watching, but now the watchmen are keeping tabs on me too. I was so stupid to trust any of these people. *They are all insane.* I wonder if I can make the horse run if I asked it to.

"Things need to change," he whispers. "I've been fighting ever since I first laid eyes on your grandmother, but my life is winding down and I haven't been able to do enough. I need those willing to carry on after I am gone."

"Carry on with what?" I can't help the rising panic in my voice. I want to make the horses stop walking so I can look at his face, but I don't dare pull on the reins.

"Everything has been too small. I'd hoped to see an end to all of this," he waves his hand, gesturing to the open fields around us, "while I was still alive, but I don't think that's going to happen."

"You want to destroy the earth?" I ask, horrified, and seriously concerned about his mental stability.

"No," he laughs. "I want to destroy the wall."

This is the most refreshing thing I've ever heard in my life. I drink these words in, too stunned to speak. We ride over a hill and come to a forest. Evergreen pines stretch for miles in either direction. Atlas casts a worried look to me, like all this came too soon.

"Will you help?" he asks quickly.

"Oh yes." I smile. "What do you need me to do?"

"You even sound like her sometimes." He shakes his head in wonder. "The strength in your voice is hers. Genetics are a curious thing. I think there was a reason I met her and I think this reason is you." He pulls against the reins so that his horse stops and Pegasus comes to a halt beside him.

"First, I need to figure out who is attacking us and how to stop them. Don't worry too much about this, I'll figure out a way. I know you want to help but if they don't agree to fight it isn't the end of the world."

"Then why did you agree to let me come?" I ask in confusion.

"Because I needed to meet you." He smiles. "And if you can convince them, it will help. But I don't see that happening. They have no reason to fight alongside us. What I need from you is inside of the wall. I've fought too long on the outside, beating my fist against the iron gates. It's time to try a new approach. We have to bring the wall down from within."

My eyes open wide and I want to protest, but he places a finger over his lips, directing his eyes to the tree line. "We'll have more time to talk of this later. First, we need to save our home and then we need to fix it."

*

The forest feels alive. The evergreen branches give color to the world again. Atlas rides ahead of me now, there's not enough room for the horses to walk side by side, and I'm left alone with my racing thoughts.

What can I do inside the wall? My paintings aren't going to change anything. My stomach is in knots. *Did I really think that going home meant I would get to stay there?* Maybe that was a foolish dream. I'll have to be okay with seeing them a final time and letting them know that I'm alright. That'll have to be enough. *But it's not what I wanted.* No, it's not.

What exactly does he plan to do and what has he done to change anything? He's a watchman. He could have just told everyone the truth and they would have demanded the gates be opened. Mother Auburn's voice is suddenly in my head, *You'll bring destruction to them.*

This is all a chaotic, confusing mess. I stare at Atlas' back screaming unanswered questions at him. But if I've learned anything in my short time in this world, it's to be careful with what I say. If he is worried someone is listening then I should be too. By the time the forest thins out, I've already made up my mind. I'll do whatever needs to be done to tear down the wall. I am not a coward.

*

I can smell the sea. I can't see it, but I can smell it. My heels dig into Pegasus' side as I unconsciously will him forward. The horse responds by going faster and I cry out as Atlas grabs his reins.

"Whoa there, buddy," he soothes the beast.

My heart pounds against my chest. "Are we almost to the ocean?"

"The ocean?" Humor lights up his face. "Can you taste it on the wind?" I nod deliriously, sucking in gulps of air like I can't breathe.

Atlas laughs. "Don't get your hopes up too soon. I promise you'll see the ocean, but for now we are going to the bay. It's brackish water."

Brackish. I know that word. It's where fresh water merges with the sea. I'll take it anyway. This means I'm one step closer to going home.

✝ CHAPTER FOURTEEN ✝

The shipyard is not at all what I imagined. It's a city of its own. Large metal cranes climb to the sky, towering over the broken remnants of the massive ships the watchmen sail on. I almost thought it would be like our harbor, but it's more like a wrecking yard. *A really, really big wrecking yard.* It's a city that masquerades as a graveyard of ships gutted and torn. But there is so much life here, so much noise, as the cranes screech and men all dressed in the watchmen's uniform yell to one another. *This must be where the watchmen are born.* And beneath all this chaos, the muddied scent of fresh salt air alights my every sense.

"Are you happy?" Atlas stands beside me. We left the horses in the barn and although my legs ache in ways I can't define, I'm so giddy from seeing these ships here that I can't wipe the smile from my face.

"What are they doing?" The question isn't specific, I want to understand every part of this place.

"These are the remains of naval vessels from long ago," Atlas explains solemnly. "Some we harvest for parts and the others we try to make work again."

"What's that?" I point to the smokestack rising from a distant building. It isn't a dome, it's square and made out of rusted metal. The familiarity of the design makes me sigh in happiness.

"The weapons facility." He starts walking away.

It takes me a lifetime to peel my eyes from the scene. Beyond the ships is water, a vast expanse of brackish water, but it sure looks like the sea. If I dove from the pier, I could swim to it.

"I'll take you to the barracks room so you can rest and relax," he says. But I don't want to rest. The moisture in the air coats my skin, easing the dryness I've become accustomed to since coming ashore. It energizes me. I just want to be back out on the water now. "Come on, Brooke. There's someone I want you to meet."

*

The metal door bangs shut behind me, blocking out the sight of the bay. Atlas raises his chin and walks with purpose down the hall. This building smells musty, old and worn, with the faintest hint of something citrus. The hallway walls are bare, just empty space wiped clean.

Down the hall, past the closed metal doors, we enter a common room. A group of watchmen engaged in various tasks all snap to attention when Atlas enters. All but one.

"You're back early." A man with black unruly hair sits alone at the table shuffling the cards that were discarded by the other men when they jumped to attention. His gaze flicks to me and his eyes travel slowly up my body until they land on my face.

Gods, I hope I'm not blushing. His eyes are the clearest shade of ocean blue. They almost look like glass. I'm mesmerized by them. He swallows hard, his Adam's apple bobbing in his throat, and then licks his lips.

"What goddess did you bring to our shithole bay?" He gives me a mischievous smile. If I wasn't blushing before, I can guarantee I am now.

"Put on your blouse, Lopt," Atlas commands. "There's a sister in your presence."

Lopt stands and reaches for the outer layer of the watchmen's uniform that is slung over the back of his chair. He's almost as tall as Aegir or Tordon, but his body is lean and taunt against the thin material of his t-shirt.

"Can't upset our sisters now, can we?" Lopt winks as he shrugs on his blouse and then rubs his fingers through his hair.

"At ease, gentlemen." Atlas shakes his head. One of the other watchmen kicks out at Lopt from behind the table, but he easily avoids the outstretched foot and the watchman stumbles while clinging to his chair.

"Brooke, this is Lopt," Atlas says as Lopt steps forward to shake my hand. "He's a trickster, but don't let him fool you. There is a real heart in there somewhere."

"Don't tell all my secrets, old man." I can't quit staring into his eyes. They reflect the sea within them.

Quick as lightning, Atlas reaches out and smacks Lopt on the back of his head. Lopt seems momentarily surprised, before a smile turns his lips. All the other watchmen burst out laughing.

"I was distracted." Lopt shrugs.

"Or maybe I'm not that old after all," Atlas chuckles. "Now button your blouse and come with me. I need to brief the captains about this new development and since you are the most useless man here, you can escort Brooke to her room for the night."

"The whole night?" Lopt asks playfully as we step into the hall.

"Watch yourself, boy," Atlas snaps.

"I'm just teasing." Lopt holds his hands in the air. "But shouldn't we let Miss Brooke decide if she'd like the company?"

"No thank you." I roll my eyes, but I can't wipe the smile from my face. He's actually kind of funny.

"My heart." He closes his eyes and clutches at his chest.

"It's your head that's broken," Atlas sighs. "This is why we can't take you anywhere. You're lucky Brooke is who she is because a different sister wouldn't tolerate your bullshit."

"What makes me different?" I ask.

Lopt watches me in amusement as we walk down the hall. "That you're not a stuck-up land lover. My mother was a barbarian like you. I'm part barbarian too."

"You already know who I am?" I glance nervously over my shoulder like it's a secret I should be able to hide by now. I mean, I'm wearing white for gods' sakes.

"Word travels fast." Lopt winks.

"It's because I radioed him last night." Atlas grits his teeth as he marches ahead of us. "You can trust Lopt, Brooke. Even if he is an idiot."

*

"Right this way, goddess." Lopt directs me to the stairs. It's unnerving how comfortable I already feel around him. I don't even mind that we are alone.

"They won't like this plan," Lopt says. His long legs take the steps two at a time and I have to hurry to stay caught up. "Atlas is going to have his work cut out trying to convince them."

"By plan, I'm assuming me." I bite my lip. "Why won't they like this plan?"

"Because they aren't like us," he whispers conspiratorially.

"No offense," I laugh. "But I don't see what we have in common either."

"For starters, we're both ridiculously good looking."

"Oh, please." I sigh.

"Please what?" He stops walking to smile at me. "Anything you want, just ask."

I shake my head as I push past him to get to the top of the stairs. He opens the door to the right of us in the second-floor hall and closes it behind him before continuing, "They won't like the plan because they are batshit crazy."

I glance around the simple room, trying not to be nervous that it's just the two of us in this little space with only a single bed. "That's an interesting choice of words."

Lopt leans against the wall and watches me intently. "There's no other way to describe it. They hate women, that's why they choose to stay here after their contract ends. They can't stand feeling inferior to females, but they have a sick sense of morality. They think their job is important and they need to protect the earth, to keep it safe for the fragile women that live there. And they hate the savages more than women because that's something they can control. In their mind, everyone outside the wall is the enemy and everyone inside is weak."

"What makes you different from them?" I don't want to sit on the bed with him standing there, so I walk across the room to the window and sit on the windowsill.

"Oh, that's easy." He grins. "I hate everyone equally."

I can't help but laugh. "So why does it matter if they like the plan or not? Isn't Atlas in charge?"

"It's not as simple as being in charge." Lopt leans his head back against the wall. "The way of the watchmen is deep rooted in this twisted mentality. Even being in charge doesn't change everything and there are too many of them like this in leadership positions. Real change takes a lot of people to change what they believe. That's why we are going to need you if we want to tear down the wall."

The color drains from my face. Atlas, the warrior leader of the watchmen, seemed nervous to say that in the middle of an open field and here this cocky young watchman just blurts the words out.

"Sorry about that," he says, reading my expression. "This is why I'm not allowed to leave. I don't know how to mince my words and Atlas is afraid of what I'll say."

This sort of honesty is so refreshing that I want to hug him. I don't, but it seems like a nice idea.

"Well, you can't leave anyway, you're a watchman." I shrug.

"Was a watchman." He shakes a long finger at me. "My contract ended last year."

"That's horrible," I exclaim. "Don't you want to go home?"

"I am going home." He smiles mischievously. "It'll be my job to escort you on the ship and into the city on the sea to speak with the locals. Then I'm to get you safely back inside the wall. But I'll be home for a little while. You see, I don't belong here any more than you do."

*

Atlas isn't coming with us. Honestly, it seems like no one is.

"That's the problem." Lopt leans his long arms over the railing. "We don't have enough watchmen to man all these ships. Those two are destroyers like this one and they are fully operational, but they are just sitting ducks."

"Why bother to fix them?" I stare down at the pier where Atlas came to say goodbye. It grows smaller in the distance. I'll only get a few days to convince them to fight.

"After that, you'll come back and go to the university." Atlas had rubbed a fist across his tired eyes. *"That's where your real work will begin."*

"It's good for training." Lopt stretches his neck and the breeze blows back his hair as he stares at me with those piercing eyes. "That's where they teach the younger watchmen what it's like to work on a ship and how to hate those filthy savages outside the wall."

"That must have been hard." Sympathy for the boy he once was chases Atlas' cryptic words from my mind. "What did your mother think of all this?"

"She hated it until the day she died." He laughs, but I don't think it's funny. "My father Henry tried his hardest to keep her happy, but she wasn't made to live on the land."

"Wait." My jaw drops to the deck. "Henry is your father? Like the Henry who decided to bring me here?"

"Yep." Lopt smiles. "And Atlas is my great uncle. Why do you think they let me get away with being such an asshole?"

I eye him warily, shaking my head. This guy is something else.

"Come here." He grabs my hand and pulls me forward along the deck. The wind picks up, smothering the sound of my reply, but I don't think he was waiting for one anyway.

Tears well in my eyes when he takes me to the bow of the ship. The vessel seems to move slowly, but it's just an illusion. The bay quickly narrows at the open Northern Gates and we sail straight through them. Then there is nothing to see but the ocean.

She's still there waiting for me. Thousands of miles of endless horizon. Waves crashing and parting against the hull of the ship as it slices through the water. I wish I could touch it, but we are too high up. I can taste it though. The salt on my lips and the air in my lungs, this experience fills my soul with peace.

"Yeah," Lopt says softly as he stares at my face. "You weren't made to live on land either."

*

The skeleton crew works tirelessly to keep the massive vessel moving. Lopt showed me to the officers' quarters where I'll be staying on this trip and told me to relax as he rolled up his sleeves. Like an idiot, I ignored him and now I'm following him once again through the ship. I'm going to get lost in here, but Lopt moves easily through the maze of passageways and ladders, closing one heavy door before opening the next.

Before I can ask where we are going, he pushes me into the galley. The head cook watchman gives me a once over before shaking his head.

"She'll stain her clothes," the cook complains.

"Tell her that," Lopt laughs. I grab the nearest rag and tie it around my waist. Both men turn to stare at me.

"What?" I raise my hands in the air. "Problem solved."

*

It's amazing how a ship this big can feel so cramped and small. The cook named Nolan has to suck in his large belly to let me pass. Despite his earlier protest, he's grateful for the help. Or maybe he's just happy to have someone to talk to. He hasn't stopped talking since I arrived.

Nolan volunteered for this mission, leaving his wife and two daughters at home. His wife is the nurse for the university. He hopes I'll meet her one day. We work to prepare dinner for ninety-five watchmen and one woman.

I gasp when I hear that number. *Where are they all hiding?* "How many more people do they need to fight the hostiles?"

"We need three-hundred men per ship and most of our ships are at half crew," Nolan sighs.

"And we still have two destroyers sitting at the docks in the harbor."

The walls feel like they are pressing in as I imagine that many people crammed into this dining space. *How am I supposed to convince thousands of people to fight?* I feel like I need to ask Lopt for a job above deck as the weight of the ship closes in on me. Nolan must sense my worry. He pats me on the shoulder before returning to the giant pot of stew on the stove.

"It may not seem like an important job we are doing here," he confides. "When food is good, moral is high. Real strength comes within and it's my job to fuel that. This is just as important as weapons training and maintaining equipment. Sometimes all we can do is be a little, but important, part of the overall machine."

The first wave of watchmen come down to eat and I stack the trays as Nolan directs. Their eyes are downcast when they approach as if they are embarrassed to be near me. I busy myself with washing the dishes so I don't ruin their meal.

"Watchman Ladin," a man growls from the line. Nolan turns in confusion. "Why is the woman working down here?"

"She wanted to." Nolan shrugs before ladling more food into the steel metal serving bins.

I slowly look up to see a bulbous man, with a red mustache so thick it hides his upper lip, narrow his eyes at me. "Excuse me, sister, but you should be in your room. We'll have everything you need brought to you there."

"It sounds like you are undermanned," I reply quickly. "I'd be more useful if I could actually help out."

"It isn't necessary." He squares his shoulders. "We can handle things ourselves." *Curse the gods, he's one of them.*

"She doesn't listen well." Lopt is suddenly beside the watchman, appearing out of thin air. Or maybe he popped up from behind the bulkhead. There are a lot of places to disappear down here. "And she'll probably become annoying if you don't give her something to do." He winks at me and I can't help but smile.

"Atlas assured me this wouldn't be a problem." The watchman tugs at his mustache. Maybe that's how he gets it to grow so full. "Sister, your job is to convince the barbarians to man up and fight. That's the hardest job we have to give, and since we'll be there in the morning, why don't you rest to save your strength."

Tomorrow. My heart grows wings. I untie the rag from around my waist and toss it in the linen basket.

"It was nice meeting you, Nolan," I call back despite the heated glare of the mustached watchman.

"Likewise." Nolan salutes me with a wooden spoon.

*

"That watchman didn't like me," I say to Lopt once the door is closed behind us. "Is he one of the men you were talking about?"

"One of the worst," Lopt chuckles. "His name is Watchman Hall and he is the captain of this ship."

"How many watchmen are like him? Or I guess, how many are like you?" I ask.

"Now that's a question." He smiles playfully. "There are a few of us who've been fighting for change and every day more watchmen see our goals as noble ones. Thankfully, Atlas is the commander now, but a large portion of the watchmen are stuck in their archaic ways and it's been hard to break them."

"I'm starting to think I hate most people too," I sigh, trying unsuccessfully to sit on the edge of the bunk. There are three of these bunks stacked on top of each other with two feet of space between the mattresses. My stomach ties itself in knots at the thought of sleeping in this tiny box. Thinking about my comfortable bed in the Welcome Center makes me homesick in a way that disgusts me.

I decide not to think of that. "What time will we be there tomorrow?"

"We'll probably be there tonight." Lopt slides down against the wall locker and stretches his legs out on the floor before lacing his fingers behind his head. "They'll drop anchor and the ferry will be there in the morning."

I look at the mattress behind me and reassess the situation, sitting down next to him instead. The space is small but we make it work.

"What's the plan? If they see me coming in with the watchmen they'll be confused. I'm not sure how to explain that. Truthfully, I'm not sure how to explain any of this."

"Well, you're in luck." Lopt closes his eyes. "Atlas already thought of that. The watchmen aren't coming with you. No suspicion, just you doing your thing."

This revelation should bring me some relief, but I chew my lip as my pulse begins to race. "What if I fail?"

"This isn't about winning or losing. They are already expecting you to fail," Lopt mumbles with his eyes still closed. "You aren't going to let anyone down. This is just a show. The citizens felt helpless and they wanted to do something. You're their hero now and they'll welcome you back with open arms. Atlas is counting on this. I don't think he'll even tell the council the truth if the barbarians don't fight. He'll brag you up, make sure they know how hard you tried."

"Excuse me?" Anger rolls across my skin and I can't explain why. All I know is this is sickening. "Without my people, how will you fight the hostiles? How will you keep the cities safe? I can't fail if it means they are in danger."

"It'll be hard but we will manage." Lopt sighs. "Atlas has never let us down yet."

I slam my fists against the floor. *Is everything a game to these people?* "Listen, I like Atlas too, but even after what he's told me, I don't see how he's done anything great. Supposedly he's spent his whole life trying to change things. Yet thousands of people are still outside the wall believing a retirement ship will bring them to the land if they just work hard and never cause any problems."

"You can read." Lopt's beautiful eyes are suddenly open, hypnotizing me where I sit. "You could read before you came to the district. Atlas did that."

"No, he didn't." *Screw this arrogant jerk's pretty eyes.* "My father taught me to read."

"Why do you think more people aren't taught how to read?" he asks.

"Because there's no point in it," I groan in frustration. "There are no books outside the wall. No materials to document anything with."

"For someone so smart, it's hard to believe you can be this blind." He leans back against the locker.

"For a very long time, it was a punishable offense to read. The watchmen took it seriously. If the barbarians could learn, if they could educate and better themselves, then they would be harder to control. Any forward progress was stalled. Any sign of intelligence or creative ability was stamped out before it could light a fire. But Atlas changed that. He appealed to the citizens and got them to alter the archaic laws.

"Now all those mothers and sisters say they hope you'll learn how to read despite the limitations, and because your people still can't read, it just confirms their beliefs that they are superior. Then Atlas had an idea for a program to save some people who showed promise, the people who rose above their circumstances, and bring them inside the wall. My father took that one over. That's why you are so important, why it's so important to maintain this celebrity image of yours. You are proof that not all barbarians are the same. And they will want to see you. Better still, you're a woman. The council will one day listen to you. That's why this doesn't matter now and it's imperative to get you back there. You're the key to tearing down the wall and we'll be there to help every step of the way."

I sit silently, digesting this all. *Does everyone inside the wall know about this?* I think of the look on

Maisy's and the rest of the girls' faces when I asked them why they didn't think more of us could read. *Stupid, stupid, stupid.* How could I be this stupid? Of course they had ways to control us. The retirement ship is just another tool. How am I supposed to sit there and look these people in the eyes again? There are so many moving parts that I can't pick just one to understand. My heart is racing and I can't breathe.

"Do you think we could go above deck?" I whisper. "I need to see the ocean."

"Anything you want, goddess." Lopt jumps to his feet.

*

I expect Lopt to continue talking when we are alone on the deck, but he doesn't even follow me as I walk through the night to the uppermost portion of the bow of the ship. I'm grateful for that. I need the chance to think.

These people need help. *Serious help.* Is there really a way to show them they are wrong? Maybe Lopt and Atlas are right. They need to meet someone from outside the wall, someone they can connect with. Just like I connected with Calder when we spent time together. I can do it again. I'll have to swallow my pride, but if it means changing the future for my family then I think I can do it. *I have to do it for them.*

The moonlit water crashes against the hull, sending sprays of foam that cling to the metal siding before rolling back down to the ocean without ever reaching my feet. Millions of stars fill the sky with nothing to block them from view. I inhale deeply, breathing the sweet salty air from the sea. It fills my veins with more than blood. *A sense of purpose, a way to change things.* My dad would be proud of me.

Somehow in the midst of all this chaos, I've found my place in the world. They need me to help them and I can do this. There are good men hidden within the watch, even those like Calder who don't know there is a different way yet. I glance back over my shoulder, ashamed that I trusted Lopt so easily when Calder risked so much for me and it took me forever to see it.

Lopt sits aloof, his memorizing eyes watching the stars. I turn to look at them now. I wish I could paint the night sky. A million twinkling lights set against a sea of darkness and reflecting on the water below. But it's impossible. This is one of those moments where you'd have to be there to truly appreciate all the majestic glory.

And here I am in the middle of it all. A broken girl with too much pride who somehow has a real purpose in life. I can help them convince the citizens to change things and I won't have to do it alone. A smile teases my lips as I listen to the sea call out her ancient song.

"We are really going to fix it!" My dad laughed as he twirled me and Meghan around the kitchen.

Yes dad. I nod in agreement now. *I don't know how this happened or how I got here, but I promise you we are going to fix the world.*

*

Darling reader,

You don't need to know what happens next. I know I'm killing you with the cliffhangers and they are killing me too! This story can stop right now. There is hope. She has a purpose and can fix the world if she does her job. You can imagine the better life she will have, all the joy that is to come. It can end here…

It wasn't my fault that certain characters took on a life of their own and messed some things up. This is uncharted waters for me. I've never not written in a trilogy.

But if you choose to be a rebel and read the next book, I won't blame you.

I love rebels.

The Winds of Change (City on the Sea #4) link here:

https://www.amazon.com/gp/product/B09D2R3F12

If you have the time, I'd love it if you can leave me your honest review. Also, if you want to know more about Atlas and Ligeia's story, come sign up for my mailing list @ www.heatherkcarson.com where you get exclusive access to the free short story *Spinner's Song*.

Thanks for reading!

Made in the USA
Columbia, SC
13 April 2022